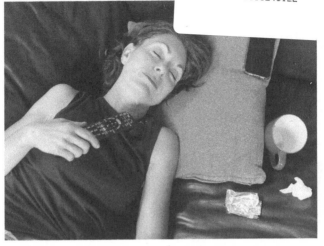

Kerri Sackville is an Australian author and columnist. She lives in the Eastern Suburbs of Sydney with her kids and a cat, and enjoys clutter, eating takeout and taking long naps on the couch. Find her on Twitter and Instagram @KerriSackville and Facebook.com/Kerri.Sackville.

Also by Kerri Sackville:

Out There: A Survival Guide for Dating in Midlife

The Little Book of Anxiety: Confessions from a Worried Life

When My Husband Does the Dishes: A Memoir of Marriage and Motherhood

the life-changing magic of

magic of

A LITTLE BIT OF MESS

the life-changing magic of A LITTLE BIT OF MESS

Kerri Sackville

HarperCollins*Publishers*

HarperCollins*Publishers*

Australia • Brazil • Canada • France • Germany • Holland • India
Italy • Japan • Mexico • New Zealand • Poland • Spain • Sweden
Switzerland • United Kingdom • United States of America

First published in Australia in 2022
by HarperCollins*Publishers* Australia Pty Limited
Level 13, 201 Elizabeth Street, Sydney NSW 2000
ABN 36 009 913 517
harpercollins.com.au

A catalogue record for this book is available from the National Library of
Australia.

ISBN 978 1 4607 6091 8 (paperback)
ISBN 978 1 4607 1401 0 (ebook)

Cover design by Andy Warren, HarperCollins Design Studio
Cover images by istockphoto.com
Author photograph by Michael Beder
Internal illustrations by Saachi Owen
Typeset in Bembo Std by Kirby Jones
Printed and bound by CPI Group (UK) Ltd, Croydon, CR0 4YY

For Kylie, a person living bravely with neatness

CONTENTS

PART TWO: A GUIDE TO DOMESTIC
   IMPERFECTION

AN APOLOGY FROM THE PUBLISHER

DEAR READER,

Many of you will have seen our promotional material for a forthcoming inspirational book on home management. It was advertised in our newsletter late last year as a 'New domestic Bible from one of this country's most inspirational women'.

You may therefore be surprised and confused to see that we at HarperCollins have published this book, *The Life-changing Magic of a Little Bit of Mess*, instead of, say, *How to Sanitise Your Home Using Only Water and a Positive Mindset*, or *The Transformational Power of Throwing All Your Things Away*, or *Heal Your Pain with Housework*.

To clarify, the book you are holding in your hands is the result of a very slight error on the part of one of our junior editors, whose name we cannot print due to ongoing litigation. You see, just over a year ago, we at HarperCollins became enamoured of the work of a prominent social-media influencer in the aspirational home-management space. This influencer – who

1

home-schools her seven children while running her multi-million-dollar kale juice business – shot to fame when photos of her stunning, all-white house and breathtaking glass pantry went viral.

With an Instagram following of over two million, this influencer is one of the leading voices of domestic artistry in the country. We at HarperCollins were keen to offer her a book deal, so that she could bring her message of attainable perfection to a new audience keen to live their best lives in their most pristine homes.

Unfortunately, this influencer has a rather similar-sounding name to another media personality, Kerri Sackville, a 'lifestyle' writer with a significantly smaller following. In a deeply regrettable mix-up, the junior HarperCollins editor charged with approaching the influencer accidentally approached Ms Sackville instead. (We are legally obliged to note that this editor was severely exhausted after staying up all night reorganising her pantry.) By the time we realised the junior editor's mistake, Ms Sackville had signed the book contract.

Now, Kerri Sackville is a competent writer, but she is not what one would call 'inspirational', particularly when it comes to the realm of home management. It is well documented that Kerri destroyed her own oven in her first and only attempt to clean it, did a television interview from her bedroom with her wardrobe door open and her bras in full view, and once had a serious weevil infestation in her kitchen. We at HarperCollins champion writers who make all sorts of life choices but, really, no one aspires to have weevils.

Still, the contract was signed, and we are legally obliged to publish, so here is Kerri's book. The junior editor has since left HarperCollins and is selling her own range of bespoke Mason jars. As for the inspirational influencer with the white house and glass pantry … well, she has deactivated her Instagram account after a plagiarism scandal involving hashtags and pantry liners, so it's probably all for the best.

A NOTE FROM THE AUTHOR

I WAS SURPRISED and delighted to be asked by HarperCollins to write an inspirational book on home management. To be honest, until I was approached by the HarperCollins editor, I hadn't considered myself to be an inspirational writer. More specifically, I hadn't considered myself to be an inspirational *person*. I haven't donated a kidney, or climbed Everest on one leg, or raised millions of dollars for charity, or saved a child from a speeding train. (I did once rescue a baby who had fallen out of his pram, but it was my own baby, and he fell out because I'd forgotten to strap him in, so I'm fairly sure that doesn't count as heroic.)

I've certainly not regarded myself as inspirational on the domestic front. My attitude to housework can best be described as 'relaxed', although my family use a slightly different term. I have a high tolerance for mess, I take a lot of naps, and – in the spirit of full disclosure – I have had weevils in my kitchen.

Still, one woman's shame is another's inspiration. The visionary HarperCollins editor, a lovely young woman called ███████████, saw something in me that I hadn't even seen in myself. In her initial email to me last year she wrote: 'I admire how you juggle work with the demands of a large family and still maintain an aspirational Instagram account.'

Initially I was confused – I mean, my family isn't that large – and I wondered if perhaps she was confusing me with someone else. But then I reviewed my entire Instagram history, and I began to see myself through ███████████'s eyes. The photos include:

- Me looking bemused in front of my recently exploded oven.
- Me posing for a selfie in my shambolic kitchen.
- Me staring sadly at a shattered bottle of wine.
- Me doing a live TV interview via Zoom with my wardrobe door open and my bras on full display.
- Me asleep, dribbling slightly, on the couch in the middle of the day.
- My cat in a sink (not relevant to this narrative, but it's an adorable pic).

Viewed separately, these are just a few cute snapshots. Viewed together, I realised, they form a cohesive and subversive narrative. My Instagram photos tell a profound and rousing story of cheerful imperfection. They reflect a philosophy of mediocrity that is eminently attainable. They celebrate the fallible, the disorganised and the incomplete.

This, I am sure, is what resonated so strongly with ███████████ from HarperCollins. This is what led her to offer me a book contract and resulted in this text you now hold in your hands. (At least, I think this is what resonated with ██████████. I haven't been able to confirm this, as she left the publisher shortly after I signed my contract, and her number is disconnected, and I haven't heard from her since.)

Either way, I am honoured to have been offered this platform from which to inspire and support others. I welcome you all to my world of domestic deficiency. I welcome you to near enough, good enough and OK. I welcome you to putting off today what you can do tomorrow!

I welcome you to the life-changing magic of a little bit of mess.

PART ONE

THE JOY OF MESS

I clean, therefore I am

The turning point

I was ten years old, and I was at my friend Leah's place. I'd played at Leah's house many times, but this was my first sleepover, and I was excited.

Leah's house, I noticed, was extremely neat. It was much neater than mine. My house was clean enough and tidy enough, but 'enough' was the operative word. My parents both worked full-time and our house was cluttered and relaxed, and I very much liked it that way. I could leave a toy out in the living room in the morning, and it would still be there in the afternoon when I got home from school.

This was not the case at Leah's house. Her living room was immaculate. The entire two-storey house was spotless, and more than a little intimidating. Her mother, Barbara Buckman, was a 'homemaker', and constantly bustled around in the background. She carried baskets of laundry, wiped down already gleaming surfaces and constantly plumped the throw cushions. I was extremely careful not to spill my juice on their white laminex table, though I needn't have worried because Barbara whisked my drink away before I'd even finished it.

When I used Leah's bathroom, I saw that the towels were folded into perfect, fluffy squares. Gosh, I thought, people fold their towels? The towels in my bathroom were slung carelessly on the rails. Sometimes my sister and I even left them on the floor!

'Want some milk?' Leah asked me as we climbed into our pyjamas. Her double bed was made up with sheets and blankets with hospital corners. My bed had a duvet that was tossed aside each morning.

'Sure,' I said.

We trooped downstairs and, as I entered the kitchen, I was surprised by what I saw. The kitchen table was set as if for a dinner party, although the entire Buckman family had eaten dinner two hours before.

'Are your parents having people over?' I asked Leah as I looked admiringly at the table. There were fancy plates and silver cutlery and china cups and linen napkins and a white porcelain jug.

Leah squinted at me. 'It's for breakfast,' she said.

'You're going to eat breakfast at night?'

Leah looked at me with pity. Clearly I was not very bright. 'No,' she said slowly, as if speaking to a toddler. 'It's for breakfast tomorrow morning.'

'But why is it all out on the table now?'

Poor Leah probably thought she'd made a mistake inviting me over. 'Mum sets it every night after we finish dinner. Doesn't your mum do that too?'

I was astonished. 'Um, sure,' I said. 'Yes. Of course she does.' My mum did not set the breakfast table at night. My mum did not set the breakfast table *at all*.

When I would wander into the kitchen wanting breakfast, Mum would wish me good morning and gesture towards the pantry. I would grab a box of Corn Flakes, take out a bowl and a spoon, pour some Corn Flakes in the bowl and add a splash of milk from the fridge. I would take my bowl to the couch in the living room, where my sister would be eating her Rice Bubbles in front of the TV. That was breakfast in our neat-enough household. It did not involve a porcelain jug.

I lay in Leah's spare bed that night thinking about the breakfast table. It was truly a revelation. Mrs Buckman had shown me a way of doing things that I didn't even know existed. Leah had told me that her mother was descended from Russian royalty, and that made perfect sense. Clearly Mrs Buckman had brought the benefit of her superior aristocratic heritage to the management of her home.

I knew right then that I was at a turning point in my life. I was used to a home that was neat and tidy, but Mrs Buckman elevated housework to another level. To Mrs Buckman, cleaning wasn't a chore: it was a calling. Mrs Buckman taught me that a person (most likely a female person) could take great pride in domestic artistry. I could be like my mother, and do just enough, or be like Mrs Buckman, and do things perfectly. When I grew up, I too could fold my towels into fluffy squares, set the table for breakfast and tuck my bedsheets into hospital corners.

Nope, I thought as I settled down to sleep, that's not for me.

It all seemed like far too much trouble for little reward. In that moment, in Leah Buckman's spare bed, I chose mess.

Editor's note: According to our fact-checker, Barbara Buckman was Bulgarian, not Russian. Her father was a shoemaker, and her mother a maid. Perhaps this is where she learned the hospital corners.

The Barbaras

When I was growing up in the 1970s and 80s, there were no social-media influencers in the home-management space. There were no social-media influencers in any space because there was no such thing as social media. There were passionate homemakers, nearly all of them women, but they were cruelly denied the opportunity to share their #homeinspo handiwork with the world.

Imagine the frustration felt by these poor women. If they colour-coded their wardrobes, or bought new linen, or decanted all their spices into matching glass jars, there was no platform on which to flaunt these achievements to other people. They could invite guests over to marvel at their wardrobe, but this was a slow and ineffective way to reach the masses. They could take artistic photos of their spice jars using their analogue cameras, then pay to develop the photos at a lab, paste the photos into a Spice Jar Album and show the album to their friends at parties, but this would be quite unspeakably weird. There were certainly no forums on which to post artfully filtered photos, or to write inspiring hashtags like #homesweethome or #cleaningmotivation or #minimalistlyfe.

Also, hashtags hadn't been invented yet.

If Barbara Buckman was a young mum in our internet age, there is every chance her groundbreaking breakfast-setting routine would have gone viral. Barbara would have her own Instagram account and blog, something like *Barbara's World* or *The Organised Barb* or *Let's Watch Barbara Clean*. She would write a weekly newsletter offering tips on the best butter knives, and on what toaster to buy, and how make organic jam. She would make TikTok tutorials about the various ways to set a breakfast table.

'Keep those knives and forks parallel!' she would say briskly, her backcombed hair in a perfect pompadour. 'Equidistant from the table's edge. No finger marks on the glasses!'

Eventually, one of her TikToks would be noticed by a television producer and Barbara would secure a guest spot on a morning show, talking about the importance of well-placed cutlery. This would lead to a five-figure deal for a book called *The Barbara Edit,* or *Make Breakfast with Barbara,* or *The Life-Changing Magic of Setting the Table the Night Before.* Barbara would eventually have her own line of breakfast foods – a range of kale-infused juices, a low-sugar jam and a gluten-free, organic muesli. She would certainly have her own dedicated hashtag, something like #setyourtablewithBarb, #Barbsfamilybreakfast or #girlwashyourplate.

Within weeks of her book hitting the bestseller list, the Barbara Effect would take hold. Women around the country would be setting their breakfast tables at night, buying expensive ceramic bowls and decanting their cornflakes into Mason jars. And then people like my mum – who ate her piece of toast at the sink – would feel slightly inadequate and ashamed.

For Leah's sake, and mine, I'm glad none of this happened.

These days, of course, there are Barbaras everywhere, and they all have their own #homeinspo platforms. There are cleaning Barbaras, decluttering Barbaras, home-organisation Barbaras and pantry-designer Barbaras. They run websites, blogs, Facebook groups and Subreddits, and they send out newsletters about grout brushes and flatware. They have Instagram, YouTube and TikTok accounts with names like *Declutter with Wendy*, *Scrub Mama* and *Ladies Who Clean*. They share laundry tips, housework schedules, cleaning advice and stain-removal hacks. They post photographs of their immaculate homes, their minimalist capsule wardrobes and their beautifully organised pantries.

Some of the Barbaras are relatable and seem like regular human beings, albeit human beings who are unusually passionate about folding fitted sheets and removing soap scum from the shower. Other Barbaras are rather less relatable, and live in impeccable homes with multiple children who do not seem to generate mess. One high-profile influencer home-schooled her seven attractive kids, ran a business selling kale juice and lived in a pristine white house. She has since gone offline so I can't direct you to her account, but a white house? How did she do it? I once bought a white couch and it was stained within a month, and that was before I had kids.

Relatable or not, the Barbaras share one thing in common: they are, almost without exception, female. There is no blog to be found named *Dude who Loves Laundry*, no Instagram account for @DeclutterMan. There is no TikTok profile called @BruceLovestoClean, nor a Facebook group for *Fathers Who Mop*. It's possible that there are men who love polishing their skirting boards, but they just don't post about it on the socials. Perhaps there is a flourishing community of *Men Who Love Cleaning* in anonymous chat rooms on the dark web? Perhaps they are furtively discussing mould removal and cobweb brooms, away from the prying eyes of us women?

A romp through cleaning advice

Casting my eye over the plethora of #homeinspo advice online, I realised that I have been naïve. I always believed housework was a relatively simple, if deeply monotonous affair. You put stuff away in cupboards. You change the sheets once a week. You wipe the surfaces when they're sticky and mop the floors when they're gross. You vacuum the carpets when someone in your household starts to sneeze and you clean out the fridge when the uneaten veggies begin to fizz. You throw a bucket of bleach at the toilet when it's in crisis, and deal with it as quickly and as rarely as you can.

I was wrong. It turns out that housework requires considerable expertise. I had underestimated the breadth of skills required to clean and tidy one's home.

There are more books on housework than I could count, let alone read, let alone dust if they were stacked on my shelf. I have browsed through books on how to clean a home systematically, books on how to clean a home cheaply, books on how to clean a home organically and books on how to clean a home when you have kids. (These latter books presumably outline various ways to get your kids to move out of the house.)

I skipped the sub-genre of books on Christian cleaning, which teach the faithful to establish their homes as Houses of Glory and Houses of God. I can't be bothered tidying up for my human visitors; I certainly don't have the energy to ready my house for the Lord. (Also, I'm Jewish, so probably not the target audience, but that's beside the point.)

Happily, I found my niche in the books on speed cleaning – really the only type of cleaning that excites me. I spent many a happy hour lying on my couch eating chocolate and marvelling at how quickly I could clean my house.

The first book I read offered me a foolproof system to clean my house in just fifteen minutes a day. This felt suspiciously fast, as it takes me at least four minutes to wrestle the vacuum cleaner out of the laundry, and another three minutes to be able to walk again after I drop it on my foot.

When I picked up the next book, I felt a little ripped off, as I learned that fifteen minutes isn't fast at all. This next book promised I could clean my home in just ten minutes a day, which is a whole thirty-three per cent faster! I'd have to clean at one and a half times my normal speed though, and this seemed gruelling. Still, I had already saved five minutes of my time, and I hadn't even picked up a sponge.

Well, a ten-minute speed clean seemed positively leisurely when I picked up the next book in the pile. This one guaranteed me a spotless home in eight minutes flat, which seemed more than a little improbable. By the time I recovered from my vacuum-induced injuries, I'd have sixty seconds left to transform my home.

I didn't bother reading the remaining book, because I knew it couldn't live up to its promise. This final book promised me a tidy home in 'less time than you imagine', which was obviously not going to happen. I was already imagining cleaning my home in eight minutes, so how much less time could it take? Could I tidy my house is just six minutes? Four minutes? Two? Perhaps I could look at the house in a very stern manner and the dirt would feel intimidated and leave?

I continued my research, trawling through blogs and forums discussing every possible approach to cleaning. I did not actually clean – that wasn't in my publishing contract – but I did read a great deal about housework. I learned:

- One does not simply spray all-purpose cleaner on a blotch, give it a little wipe and hope for the best. There is an entire body of knowledge addressing every possible type of blemish, from red lipstick on your duvet to gunpowder on your cream leather couch; from scratch marks on your wooden floors to bloodstains on your shagpile carpet.
- For people who prefer housework to be as difficult as humanly possible, there are books and websites that outline how to make low-toxicity cleaning products from scratch. (Spoiler alert: they all contain the same two ingredients, vinegar and bicarb soda.)
- Mops and vacuums are just starter tools! Committed #homeinspo influencers use complex equipment like Three-In-One Crosswaves and Cordless Turbo Mops and Multi-Function Floor Cleaners and Heavy-Duty Steam Systems, right alongside their home-made detergents. (As a side note: I don't mean to disparage either

vinegar or bicarb, but perhaps if these people used commercial cleaning sprays instead of salad dressing, they wouldn't need the horsepower of expensive machines?)

- There is an entire subgenre of cleaning videos for those who prefer an extended cleaning session, and apparently, inexplicably, there are those who do! Just google 'marathon cleaning' and you can enjoy watching one-hour, six-hour, eight-hour, even *two-day* cleaning sessions, all streamed for your viewing pleasure. (I'd gain significant satisfaction from watching a stranger clean *my* house. I'd pay for the privilege, and indeed I have. But the desire to watch strangers clean their *own* homes leaves me quite profoundly confused.)

Throw out everything you own

There are many different approaches to home organisation, each outlined by experts and proselytised by devotees. But all the approaches have one sacred tenet in common: you need to throw out absolutely everything you own.

I exaggerate, of course. You are allowed to keep some special items. But minimalism is good, too many possessions are bad and clutter is the nemesis of your sanity and home.

Exactly which items you may keep depends on the philosophy you accept, and there are many different philosophies from which to choose. There are more books on how to declutter than there are vases in my mother's house – and my mum has never decluttered, so that is a large number indeed.

There are books with names like *Declutter with Feng Shui*, *No You Don't Deserve Nice Things* and *Throw Out 100 Things Now,* as well as the classic work *How to Live in a Bleak, Empty Home So That You Don't Inconvenience Your Kids.*

If you subscribe to the Japanese art of decluttering, you must consider each item in your house and determine whether it sparks joy in your soul. If an item brings you joy, it may stay in your home; if it doesn't, you must thank it, then toss it brutally in the bin.

I like the idea of thanking possessions, because I am easily bored, and it's nice having something to talk to. On the other hand, I have an extremely low threshold for irritation, so I'd need to modify my Japanese decluttering or most of my possessions would end up in the trash.

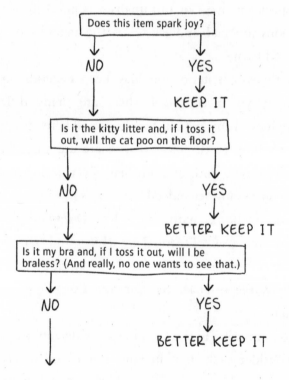

GO TO THE NEXT PAGE ↷

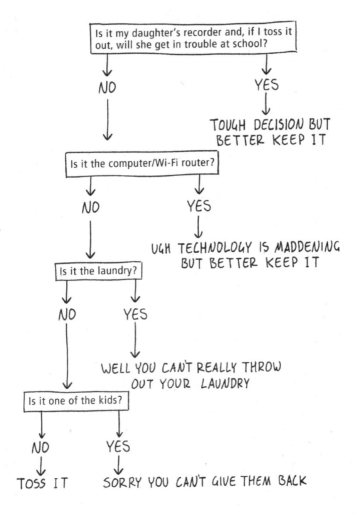

If you are a proponent of the Swedish art of death cleaning, you will need to get rid of anything that won't spark your children's joy. The Swedish art of death cleaning demands that you throw out all your worldly goods so that your relatives won't need to do so after you die. This philosophy makes perfect sense to me when I visit my parents' home, which is filled to the brim with artworks, knick-knacks, tchotchkes, books and a variety of colourful vases. It makes rather less sense to me when I am in my own home, which is filled to the brim with artworks, knick-knacks, tchotchkes, books and a variety of miniature cows.

Now, cows are obviously much more appealing than vases, so my kids are luckier than I am. Still, should my parents live in austere minimalism simply to save me the trouble of one day cleaning out their house? Well, yes, thanks Mum, that would be great. Here, have some garbage bags. Call me when it's done.

But should *I* live in austere minimalism simply to save *my* kids the trouble of one day cleaning out my house? Not a chance, you lazy ingrates. I really love my cows.

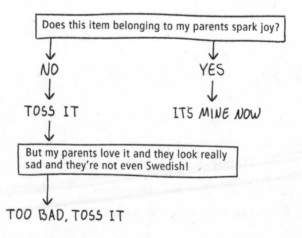

A rainbow bookshelf

If minimalism is the first tenet of home organisation, the second tenet is that your possessions should be colour-coded like a packet of Skittles – from your books to your clothes and cosmetics, from your stationery to the snack items in your pantry.

Domestic rainbows please me enormously, and colour-coding makes your stuff look soothingly ordered, in a conventional, Instagram-ready way. Having said that, your stuff will look the same as everybody else's stuff if they, too, follow these rainbow guidelines.

More importantly, colour-coding breaks the only law of home organisation, which is that you need to be able to locate things in your home. Sure, it's fine in your wardrobe, when you're trying to find your pink t-shirt, or in your art box when you're looking for the orange pencil. It works rather less well when you're searching for a snack in your pantry and don't know whether the sultana packet is red, green or blue.

And God help you when you urgently need that book on stain removal and you can't recall the colour of its spine. (Then again, you don't need a book: the answer is vinegar and bicarb. You can leave your perfect rainbow alone.)

The great unanswered question

The aspirational home-management space is large and, ironically, very cluttered. In every corner there are influencers telling you how to clean and organise your home. Their voices differ, their tips and tricks vary, but their content conveys the same message: if you use the appropriate products and potions, your home too can be spotless. If you follow the right schedule and watch the right motivational videos, you can banish all mess. If you throw out all the vases that haven't sparked joy in the past year, your home can be perfectly decluttered. (Please note: my mother insists that all of her vases spark joy, and who am I to argue?) If you fold your fitted sheets properly, stack your books in rainbow order and decant your foodstuffs into Mason jars with calligraphic labels, you too can achieve domestic perfection.

You need never be burdened by a smear on your splashback, a smudge on your bedroom window or a stain on your white duvet. You can have the perfect kitchen. The perfect wardrobe. The perfect pantry. The perfect home!

There is just one small detail that remains unclear: why does anybody *need* a perfect home?

Now, there are people who genuinely enjoy cleaning and tidying their homes. If this is you, I am delighted for you, and endorse your passion. (I also ask that you hold space for the possibility that you might enjoy cleaning *my* home, and I extend a warm invitation for you to come over and find out.)

But this book was not written for people who enjoy cleaning. This book was written for people who do *not* enjoy cleaning, or who do not prioritise cleaning, or who rank cleaning extremely low on their list of preferred activities – somewhere under Pap smears, doing tax returns and attending parent-teacher nights.

So, my domestically challenged friends, this book is here to reassure you. No matter what the influencers say, you do not need a perfect home. Imperfection is aspirational, and I shall show you why.

ONE

Nature abhors a vacuum (cleaner): debunking the myths of mess

Things influencers say

So, what makes these home-management influencers so ... influential? Why do they have so many people scrambling to colour-code their bookshelves and toss out joyless pairs of pants? Well, influencers offer all sorts of profound insights about why we should clean and tidy. Their sayings look extremely attractive when posted as inspirational memes against the background of a clear blue sky.

There's only one tiny problem with their motivational messages: they aren't actually true.

Influencers say things like:

'Tidy house, tidy mind.'

Well, if you've ever met someone with a perfectly tidy house, you will know this to be patently false. Most people with pristine homes are not calm and relaxed; they are extremely uptight and obsessive! (The word 'anal' springs to mind, but that seems unnecessarily disparaging, so I will not include it in this book.) It is eminently possible to have a very messy mind inside a perfectly organised home. If it was really that simple to achieve a tidy mind, there would be no need for therapists or medication. Psychologists would write us all scripts for a decluttering book and a broom, and send us on our way.

'It's just as easy to put things back in the right spot as it is to put things back in the wrong spot.'

This is demonstrably untrue, as I shall prove to you now. Go into your bedroom, pull out a t-shirt and carry it into the kitchen. Now, is it easier for you to trudge all the way back to your bedroom, or just shove the t-shirt into the pantry? Clearly, it is far easier to put things back in the wrong spot and worry about the consequences later.

'Less is more!'

OK, I concede that less can be preferable in certain circumstances: dealing with headlice, for example, or counting the wrinkles on your forehead, or contemplating the calories in a dessert. But when it comes to your home, more is generally much better. Clutter is, after all, just a plethora of possessions, and possessions are fun to have. The more clothes you own, the more outfits you can wear. The more furniture in your house, the more places you can sit! The more knick-knacks you collect, the more lovely things you can look at. And the more vases you keep, the more flowers you can display around your home. (My mum made me include that last one. To be honest, most of her vases sit empty in cupboards, but we don't need to quibble over details.)

'A clean house fosters calm.'

Yes, I suspect a clean house might foster calm. But getting that house clean in the first place – and then striving to keep it clean forevermore – can foster some pretty serious stress.

'A housework schedule makes life easier!'

Have you *seen* a housework schedule? They outline daily and weekly and monthly tasks, many of which are completely obscure and utterly unnecessary. (Seriously, who washes their walls once a week? Or polishes their toaster every Friday afternoon?) We humans have enough to deal with in this complex modern world. We might have a work deadline on Tuesday morning, followed by a dental appointment on Tuesday afternoon, followed by netball practice for one kid and parent-teacher evening for the other, and now we're supposed to clean out the fridge on Tuesday too?

'You'll always be prepared for visitors.'

No, no, no! That's the same thing as talking about getting a 'beach body' for summer. You don't need to do anything special to have a beach body; you just need to take your existing body to the beach! Similarly, you don't need to do anything to prepare your house for visitors, you just need to open the door and wave them in.

'Nothing is more satisfying than a beautifully organised pantry.'

Oh, please. There are about seventeen billion things more satisfying than a beautifully organised pantry. Sex, for example. A nap. Chocolate biscuits. Holding a newborn baby. Buying a new pair of shoes. Doing an excellent reverse park into a very tight spot. Finding a hundred-dollar note in the street.

Cleanliness is nowhere near godliness

Home-management influencers provide tips and tricks to help us elevate our homes from messy to clean. They take for granted that cleanliness is ideal and that disorder is unfortunate indeed. But what if they are all just victims of cultural propaganda? What if mess is the superior state and the benefits of neatness are fake news?

Let's start by deconstructing one of the oldest myths in the world (or at least in the history of the broom and pan). Cleanliness is not linked to godliness at all – at least, not when it comes to your home. The Bible contains no mention of neat homes, neat tents or even neat yurts for that matter. There are references in the Bible to hand washing, foot washing, ritual bathing and even wearing clean clothes, but there is absolutely nothing in the holy text about keeping a tidy house.

There is no intrinsic spiritual or moral value in tidiness. It is not linked to virtue in any way. Domestic cleanliness is not next to godliness any more than hairiness is next to wisdom, or sleepiness is next to prescience, or equanimity is next to a good sense of smell.

Having a neat and tidy home does not mean that you're a good person; it simply means that you do a lot of cleaning. Neat people aren't kinder or more charitable than messy people, although they probably know a lot more about vinegar.

What's more, being messy does not mean that you lack discipline, or that you're lazy, or even that you're disorganised. People who live in messy houses can be extremely disciplined in other areas of their lives. In fact, people with messy houses are likely to be *more* disciplined than neat people, because they don't procrastinate when they should be working by dusting the light fittings or cleaning out the pantry.

Don't believe me? Well, I can verify this to be true, because I am genuinely messy and I am also a good person. I am messy and I'm kind and caring and generous and empathic (except for first thing in the morning, before I've had my coffee). I'm messy and I'm a good friend and a devoted mother and daughter (when I am well rested, well fed and fully caffeinated). I'm messy, and I'm conscientious and very disciplined about work (as long as nothing seriously exciting is happening on Twitter).

Of course, a messy house can be a symptom of something problematic if a person is usually tidy and then suddenly stops cleaning their home. If you cannot rouse yourself to manage the simplest household tasks, you may be clinically depressed. If this is the case, please seek out support and help, and remember that things can and will improve.

In most cases, however, a messy home is just a symptom of a busy life and/or selective blindness and/or a lack of interest in vacuuming the rug. It is a stylistic choice, not a character flaw. Many fabulous and talented people embrace mess. Beyoncé is apparently very messy. Adolf Hitler was obsessively clean.

Still don't believe me? Well, individuals who demonstrate tolerance for high levels of mess have been scientifically proven to be better in every way than individuals who are extremely tidy. In their 2017 study 'The Morality of the Unwashed Dish', Snortnoble, Trubevore et al looked at a random sample of thirty-seven thousand adults between the ages of eighteen and fifty-three, and found that people who can ignore grime and disorder in their homes are more perceptive, more self-actualised and far more fun at parties than people who are obsessively neat.

There is a cultural stigma attached to being messy, which is random and unfounded and leads to unnecessary shame. We need to end the stigma! We need to throw off the shame, along with our aprons and our books on removing unusual stains. Our intrinsic value has nothing whatsoever to do with clean grouting, ordered bookshelves or how often we wash our walls. There are many ways to be a good and decent human, some of which I have helpfully outlined below.

Editor's note: For legal reasons we are obliged to point out that the study quoted in this chapter appears to be completely fabricated and that neither Snortnoble nor Trubevore exist.

How to be a good person

- Validate your friend by liking her Instagram post, even though it's just a photo of a rather ordinary plate of chocolate mousse.
- Feign interest in the photos of your friend's baby, who looks like every other baby you've ever seen, and also a little bit like a potato.
- Listen politely to your mother tell you for the third time the disgusting details of her friend Elvira's surgery to remove that pustulant growth from her leg.
- Be a graceful winner when you beat your mother at Scrabble, and don't dance around screaming, *'Take that, you big loser!'* while pumping your fists in the air.
- Perform a random act of kindness even when no one is filming it for social media.
- Have a good passenger rating on Uber.
- Be able to apologise wholeheartedly without using the word 'but'.
- Share your hot chips with the other people at the dinner table. (This one is exceptionally difficult, and I am still working on it.)
- Press the button to donate that one dollar to charity with your online purchase.

- Respond with a laughing-face emoji to every meme your friends send you, even when it's not that funny and you haven't actually laughed.
- Always answer 'No' to the question 'Does my bum look big in that outfit?', unless the person is trying to grow their bum, in which case answer 'Yes'.
- Allow other people into your lane when you're driving, even when you're in a hurry.
- Do that little wave in your car to thank other people who let you into their lane when you're driving.
- Don't publicly shame people on social media, even when they have a little meltdown at the supermarket and you have your phone with you and could totally film them.
- Keep a secret, particularly that really juicy one that all your friends would love to hear.
- Regularly check your privilege as a white person, a cis person, a wealthy person, an able-bodied person and/or a mess-adept person with curly hair.
- Helpfully outline how to be a good person in an aspirational book on home management.

A germ a day keeps the doctor away

Not only is cleanliness not next to godliness, cleanliness is not even as healthy as you might have believed. Obsessive cleaning can rid your home of germs, and – despite the fervent proselytising of Big Cleaning – this is not in your household's best interests.

We live in an extremely germophobic society. The media has waged a relentless war against the humble germ, and a certain recent catastrophic global pandemic has not helped to improve its image. The cleaning industry has been instrumental in spreading anti-germ propaganda, intent on selling disinfectant sprays, antiseptic wipes, antibacterial soaps and hand-sanitising gels. (To be fair, though, during the certain recent catastrophic global pandemic, hand-sanitising gel was really very useful.)

If you are a germophobe, you need to forgive yourself – it is not your fault that you are biased against germs. You have been raised with the cultural stereotype of the malevolent germ, who throws rave parties in your kitchen, riots in your bathroom, and orgies with other germs in your bed. You have been shown advertising campaigns depicting evil killer germs gathering in corners of your house discussing plans for your family's annihilation. You have been taught to be constantly vigilant, wielding your disinfectant spray like a weapon, lest an army of germs runs out under cover of darkness and eats you in your sleep.

You need to confront these cruel stereotypes and learn the truth about germs: they are not all the murderous microscopic creatures you believed them to be. You do not need to de-germ your house morning and night. Germs are not all bad. #NotAllGerms.

Obviously, some germs are less equal than others. No one is suggesting that you play with a stranger's used tissues, or drink water from your toilet bowl, or lick a knife that has been used to debone raw chicken. And clearly, during a catastrophic global pandemic, it is an excellent idea to step up your hand-washing regime. In regular non-pandemic times, however, we need regular contact with dirt and germs to build our natural defences against disease.

Yes, some germs can make you sick, but too little of a bad thing can also be dangerous. We all need exposure to microbes – those bacteria, fungi and viruses collectively known as 'germs' – to develop strong, functioning immune systems.

Research has shown that exposure to friendly bacteria can help prevent diabetes, infections and allergic conditions. (I did not conduct this research. I am but a humble aspirational home-management influencer.) And an overly sanitised home environment can kill off the diverse microbiome needed to keep you and your family healthy.

Germs have been relentlessly targeted and demonised by Big Cleaning in order to encourage you to buy products that you really don't need. All those disinfectant sprays and antiseptic wipes and antibacterial soaps are not only unnecessary, they may actually be counter-productive. Anti-germ cleaning products are designed to provide solutions to problems that don't exist, much like vaginal steamers, pre-peeled bananas, egg-cracking devices and tiny shoes for dogs.

Apparently, however, there are many people who are sceptical of science, and who take the word of influencers over those of scientists and doctors. This has bothered me in the past, as I am a firm believer in science, but now that I am an influencer it suits me very well.

So, for those of you who are science sceptics, here is some hard evidence – from an influencer – that germs are good:

Personal influencer testimony (not scientifically valid)

Around twenty-two years ago, I gave birth to my first child, a baby boy. This boy was very handsome and very smart – a detail which is not at all relevant to this story, but it's my book, so I get to throw it in.

Throughout his childhood, my son was largely protected from germs. I was young then, and very energetic, and extremely scared of accidentally killing my baby. I sterilised all of his bottles for at least three minutes at a time. I washed all of his clothes in antibacterial detergent. I fed him only freshly prepared food; though, as I am a very poor cook, this was usually just mashed banana.

Two years later, I gave birth to my second child, this time a baby girl. The child was very beautiful and extremely talented, which is also not relevant but nice to know anyway.

My daughter was exposed to a wider range of germs than her older brother. I was too busy to use the steriliser, so I just gave her bottles a good wash in the sink. I ran out of antibacterial detergent and used regular laundry liquid on her clothes. I couldn't be bothered mashing bananas and fed her leftovers from my son's dinners.

Fast-forward another six years, and I had yet another child. This baby was also a girl, and she had very big eyes and an extremely loud voice. (She was also smart and beautiful and talented, but the loud voice is what people noticed first up.)

By this stage, I had realised how robust the human child can be – and besides, I was completely exhausted. I gave the baby bottles a cursory rinse under the tap before I wearily filled them with milk. I washed her clothes as rarely as possible, wiping off the worst of the filth with a wet cloth. I fed my daughter food that had fallen on the floor and, once, a mildewed biscuit that I found in the car. I wouldn't have recognised a can of disinfectant if it had jumped up and sprayed her in the face.

And here is the moral of my personal story: all three kids are absolutely fine. The germ-free one, the mildly germy one, and even the one absolutely rolling in germs. They are all healthy and well and thriving in the diverse microbiome that is our home.

We all need to confront the germophobic culture in which we live and address our unconscious bias against the persecuted germ. Germs can be toxic, yes, but so can many people, and we don't remove all humans from our environment! (Except, of course, during the recent catastrophic global pandemic, but that isn't relevant right now.)

When you embrace the life-changing magic of a little bit of mess, not only will you be healthier, you will become a more tolerant and open-minded person. Germs may be microscopically small, they may be useless at conversation, and they may not have much of a personality, but they are living creatures and they walk (or rather, float) among us. We all just need to learn to get along.

Entropy

It is important to note that people who dislike cleaning do not necessarily dislike clean houses. You can hate the verb but passionately love the adjective.

If I won a great deal of money in a lottery, the second thing I would do is hire a full-time cleaner. (The first thing I would do is buy a Chanel Classic Flap Bag in black. Check it out on Google – it's gorgeous.) The cleaner would do all the house cleaning and the laundry, tidy the kitchen after my private chef had cooked my meals and assist my personal butler to turn down my sheets and lay a chocolate on my pillow each evening. (No, I haven't given this future lottery win much thought. Why do you ask?)

Still, as much as I would enjoy a spotlessly clean house, I enjoy *not* cleaning it far more. Having a pristine home is simply not worth the time and energy required to achieve it. Though I am prepared to work hard for the important things in life, like writing books and finding the best chocolate biscuits, I am not prepared to put the same effort into things that are purely cosmetic.

(This philosophy extends to my body as well as my home. Sure, if I woke up tomorrow with ripped abs and a round bum, I'd be absolutely delighted. I'd probably buy some crop tops and do a photoshoot for Instagram. But if I need to do sit-ups or lift weights or go to the gym to get there, I'll just stick with the body I have.)

You do not need to exert the effort it would take for your home to be perfect, because your home doesn't *need* to be perfect. Your home does not need to be perfect because your home is occupied by human beings, and human beings are, by definition, imperfect. If you weren't imperfect, then you would not be a human being. You would be a robot, or a tape measure, or the laws of physics, or a straight line, and it would be hard to make a cup of tea or mop the floors if you were a straight line.

Even if your home *became* perfect, it wouldn't stay that way for long. Cleaning your home is, quite literally, a battle against the forces of nature. According to the scientific principle known as the Second Law of Thermodynamics (so named because the First Law of Thermodynamics was already taken), the universe is constantly moving towards entropy – a state of disorder, randomness and chaos. On a domestic scale, this means that your house is constantly moving towards mess, disrepair and decay. (On a global scale, this means we're all hurtling into the sun, but that isn't important right now.)

Fighting your home's inextricable progression towards entropy takes an enormous amount of energy. Every single time you get up to clean, you are engaged in a war with the laws of physics. It is exhausting, it is demoralising, and it is an exercise in futility. By tomorrow there will be new grime in the kitchen, a new smudge on the windowpane, another towel to be washed. In the battle of human being versus nature, the human will always lose.

What's more, even if you achieve a fleeting moment of domestic nirvana, it will not guarantee you contentment or self-esteem. True joy doesn't come from a glistening shower screen; it comes from within your soul (and from watching reunion videos on Instagram, eating chocolate biscuits and buying cute shoes online). Perfectionism certainly won't make you happy. I know this because I have had extensive personal experience reading up about perfectionism and it sounds very unpleasant.

Now, I'm not arguing that you should shun cleaning altogether and wallow in your own filth in a dust-coated, mouldy home. I embrace mess and imperfection, not maggots and mildew! There are basic standards of hygiene to maintain, and fungal infections are surprisingly hard to shake.

But I firmly believe it is perfectly fine to have a perfectly imperfect home. A little bit of mess is just a harmless by-product of your gloriously imperfect human life.

A time and a place for perfection

Now, just because I reject the standards of domestic perfection does not mean that I am opposed to perfection in other areas of life. There is a time and a place for perfection!

Certain things do need to be perfect or the whole world will fall apart. Tape measures, for example. Speedometers. The laws of physics. Anti-hacking software. Straight lines.

There are also tasks that need to be performed perfectly or our own lives will fall apart. I'm talking about car registrations. Home insurance. Tax returns. Inputting your credit card details so that you can buy pink pleather pants from your favourite online store. Completing the 'request a refund' form so that you can return those pleather pants when they arrive three days later and you're sober.

Then there are things that need to be perfect so that you can manage to stay alive. You want hydraulic lifts to be perfect so you don't go plummeting to your death. You want air traffic control to be perfect so that your plane stays up in the air. You want your tonsillectomy to be perfect so that you're not left with bits of tonsil in your throat. (Trust me. You don't want to go through the hell of an adult tonsillectomy, only to be told that 'near enough is good enough'.)

Finally, there are those things that aren't life-threatening, per se, but are crucial for your emotional wellbeing. These are the things that should be perfect, because if they are not, your life really will be a little bit worse.

List of things that should be perfect (non-exhaustive)

- Your morning cup of coffee. If your beverage isn't right, the entire morning is ruined, and you may as well just go back to bed until tomorrow.

- The ripeness of an avocado when you cut it. If you get in just a fraction too early or, worse, a day too late, the disappointment and regret are searing.

- The firmness of your mattress. Without a good night's sleep, there is no good day. Your windows may be sparkling, your benchtops may gleam, but if your mattress is too lumpy, too soft, or too hard, you might as well be living in a barn.

- The softness of your pillow. See above.

- The apology from that person who did you wrong. The only acceptable apology is a perfect apology: one in which they say sorry, accept responsibility, do not use the word 'but', and offer a massive box of chocolates as a token of their remorse.

- Surprise reunions with loved ones after a long time apart. I watch a lot of reunion videos on Instagram and there is a definite formula: a person hides, there is a big reveal followed by a trembling hug and, finally, tears of shock and joy. When executed perfectly, these reunions are

heartwarming. When executed imperfectly –
well, I wouldn't know, because those ones don't
make it to Instagram.

- The finale of a twelve-part Netflix thriller
  with multiple twists in which you have become
  thoroughly invested. If you devote several hours
  of your precious leisure time to a new mini-
  series when you could have been watching
  predictably satisfying reruns of *Sex and the City*,
  you need and deserve a finale in which all loose
  ends are tied up, there is a new and thrilling
  revelation, a long-lost character makes a return,
  and the two characters with unresolved sexual
  tension finally hook up.
- The fit of your bra. You simply cannot function
  well when your bra is too tight, or your breasts
  are around your navel, or your nipples are
  pointing in the wrong direction.
- The delivery of a joke. A rabbi, a priest and a
  weevil walked into a pantry … oh, hang on. I
  messed it up. Let me start again. A rabbi, a priest
  and a pantry moth walked into a weevil … no,
  that's not right … Um … A rabbi and a pantry
  moth prayed to a weevil … No? Forget it. It's a
  stupid joke anyway. And I think I've made my
  point.

- The ratio of Vegemite to butter on your toast. This is, of course, two to one, in favour of the butter. This is not up for debate and I will not be entering into any correspondence on this matter.
- A first kiss. There is nothing more thrilling than a perfect first kiss, and there is nothing more deflating than a bad one.
- Your choice of checkout lane in the supermarket. Pick well and you will race through the register. Pick poorly and you will simmer with resentment for the rest of the day.
- The ending of that book you are loving. See 'Finale of Twelve-Part Netflix Thriller.'
- The amount of fizz in your Coke. The perfect Coke is one of life's simple pleasures. Too little fizz is deeply unsatisfying; too much fizz can lead to painful Fizz Burn.
- Your imaginary conversations. If you can't win an argument with an acquaintance in your own head then you have no hope of surviving interactions in the real world and should give up human contact entirely.

Editor's note: Fizz Burn is not a legitimate medical condition.

List of things that definitely do not need to be perfect (non-exhaustive)

- Your body.
- Your relationships.
- Your parenting.
- Your home.

Disclaimer

I have been informed by the HarperCollins legal team that I have been reckless in my assertion that a house never needs to be spotlessly clean and tidy, and that I am legally obliged to point out the occasions in which perfection is required.

So, to satisfy these requirements, please find below an exhaustive list of times your home really does need to be perfect:

- It is being photographed for *Vogue Living*.
- You have murdered someone inside your home and blood has been spilled and you need to get rid of all the evidence before the police arrive.
- You are a teenager and you have hosted a spontaneous gathering of seven hundred Facebook friends while your parents were away, and you need to hide all the evidence of said gathering before they return.

- You are hosting a royal wedding in your home.
- You are the author of a book titled *My Perfectly Clean Home* and you are being interviewed by a hostile investigative journalist determined to catch you out as a fraud.
- You are shooting a commercial for a new miracle cleaning spray inside your home.
- You are a contestant on a TV game show called *World's Cleanest Home* and the prize is one million dollars.
- You have a severe anaphylactic reaction to mess.

Editor's note: The staff and management of HarperCollins strongly condemn illegal gatherings and advise young people to refrain from posting invitations on Facebook.

TWO

Storm in an unwashed teacup: nobody cares about your mess

A tug of war

The pressure to keep your home perfect is both real and pervasive. From the cleaning influencers to the decluttering gurus to the #homeinspo posts to the design shows on TV, there are myriad voices constantly hammering at us all to clean our windows, throw out our knick-knacks, plump our pillows, and build a three-storey house out of recycled shipping containers on a windy cliffside in Scotland.

What's more, there are all sorts of cultural forces hounding us to constantly aim for perfection. We are told to rise to the challenge, to try as hard as we can, to give one hundred and ten per cent! Settling for 'good enough' can feel unsettling and strange, like seeing a UFO, or leaving your phone at home, or being out at the supermarket without a bra. (This last scenario is literally my worst nightmare. I am wincing just writing it down.)

So how can anyone resist these cultural expectations and stop striving for a perfectly clean house? What will happen if you relax your housework standards just a tad?

Well, the moment you stop obsessively cleaning, you will begin a downward spiral into chaos. If you fail, even once, to iron your sheets or dust your skirting boards, you will be shunned by your family and friends. If you stubbornly refuse to polish your floorboards until they gleam, your partner will leave you, within days, for someone neater. If you put off till tomorrow what you can do today, your kids may never recover from the trauma.

Oops! Oh gosh, I'm so sorry. My fingers slipped on the keyboard! That is *not* what will actually happen. Here is what will really happen if you let your standards slip:

Nothing will happen. Nothing at all.

Your world will not fall apart if there are toys on the floor and piles of dirty laundry in the hall. Your family and friends won't notice if your floors haven't been vacuumed, and if they do happen to notice, they won't care. Your partner probably won't worry about a little bit of mess, and if they do, they can clean it up themselves. And you will traumatise your kids in a hundred different ways, but leaving dishes in the sink will not be one of them.

Imagine, if you will, your housework as a tug of war. At one end there is you, with your broom and mop and vinegar; at the other end there is your household and the detritus it generates. You can keep tugging, day after day, and get nothing but sore arms and endless frustration, or you can drop your end of the rope and stop aiming for perfection. You can decide to do the bare minimum and learn to tolerate, and even embrace, a certain degree of mess.

I dropped my end of the rope long ago, and my life has turned out just fine. I have three delightful children and a moderately well-behaved cat. I have a network of wonderful friends who love me, who only occasionally ask me why all my cupboard doors are open. And I have an exciting new career as an aspirational home-management influencer, which would never have happened had I been obsessively tidy.

Editor's note: To be clear, the author should never have been an aspirational home-management influencer at all, but it appears that horse has bolted.

Things no one has said, ever

If you find yourself panicking because your house is not perfectly clean, remember that in the entire history of the known world, no one has ever said any of the following:

- 'As a ninety-eight-year-old woman looking back on my life, my one regret is that I didn't clean the light fittings more regularly.'
- 'John left me after thirty-two blissful years of marriage because I couldn't get the streaks off my kitchen splashback.'
- 'I just wish I'd spent more quality time with my steam mop when the kids were still little.'
- 'I fell in love with Lois the moment I saw her sparkling shower screen.'
- 'Mum, I don't want to play at Lily's house anymore. She's nice and we have fun but there is a finger mark on her wall.'
- 'Today we gather together to remember Roy Smith, a fine man who was killed by the limescale in his toilet.'
- 'The dinner party would have been delightful, but there was a small blue stain on the tablecloth so Richard and I couldn't enjoy ourselves.'
- 'I didn't sleep a wink last night. It was clear the sheets hadn't been ironed.'

- 'My son failed his final exams because I couldn't get the juice stains off the carpet.'
- 'My greatest accomplishment is having kept my microwave spotless for thirty-five years.'
- 'The thing I love most about my mum is the way she cleans our rangehood every day and rinses our washing machine regularly with vinegar.'
- 'Did you see Diane this morning? It's so obvious from her outfit that she hasn't decluttered her wardrobe.'
- 'Ms Jones was definitely the most qualified for the position, but I noticed a tiny crease on her shirt sleeve near her shoulder, so I gave the job to the other candidate.'
- 'I've thought about leaving Martha, but no one else knows how to get the stains off the bottom of a cassoulet pot like she does.'
- 'And this year's Nobel Peace Prize is awarded to Jenny Smith, for her superlatively clean grouting.'
- 'I was personally offended when I visited Laura's house and noticed that her bookshelves were not colour-coded.'
- 'The roast chicken was delicious – what products did you use to clean the oven?'
- 'The floor was so clean we ate off it.'

~~Please~~ DON'T excuse the mess

If you are ever tempted to apologise for the state of your home, please remember: your visitors do not care about your mess!

Of course, some visitors may notice and comment if your home is dazzlingly clean. There are people who appreciate a beautifully maintained house, just as I appreciate great cappuccino froth or a rap song that rhymes 'heavy' with 'spaghetti'.

'What magnificent colour-coded minimalism!' your guests might sigh, or 'Just look at the shine on your floors!'

And this is all very validating, but admiration for your floors doesn't translate into affection for you or enjoyment of your company. Your visitors don't care about your pristine skirting boards any more than they care about the plates in your sink or the laundry in your hall.

So, what do your guests care about? Well, I have walked into many a messy house, and I certainly don't care whether the splashback is clean. I care about how welcome I am made to feel in the home, and how enthusiastically I am greeted at the door. I care about whether I am invited to stay for a chat, and whether I am offered a nice cup of tea. I care about whether the person has any interesting gossip, and whether they have any chocolate biscuits in the pantry.

None of us needs to greet visitors with the words, 'Please excuse the mess'. And I speak from experience: I used to apologise for my mess to anyone who rang the doorbell. I apologised for the mess when my place was relatively tidy, and I apologised for the mess to friends who couldn't care less. I apologised for the mess to a tradie who was there to check the fire alarm, and to a rather bemused delivery man who was bringing my groceries into the kitchen.

No longer!

Five reasons not to apologise for your mess

1. There is nothing shameful or embarrassing about mess. It is a completely natural and normal part of life, like gravity, or cravings for hot chips, or drunk texting, or nasal hair.

2. Mess doesn't inconvenience your guests at all or impact on them in any conceivable way. You are not asking your guests to wash your piles of dirty laundry or to drink tea from that unwashed cup in the sink. Your mess has nothing whatsoever to do with your visitors, unless you have invited them over to clean it up, in which case please stop talking and fetch them a broom.

3. Your mess will not cause your guests emotional distress; in fact, they will probably feel relieved. It is empowering for them to know that they're not the only ones with an untidy kitchen or a pile of shopping bags by the front door.

4. 'Please excuse the mess!' isn't even an apology. When you say, 'Please excuse the mess', you're not actually asking for forgiveness; you're conveying a message about yourself. You're saying, 'I recognise that the current state of my home isn't appropriately neat. This mess reflects a mere temporary aberration on my part, and not my lack of understanding of the domestic ideal. If you come back another time, my house will be perfect. I am usually a very tidy person!'

    Now, this may or may not be true, and your guests may or may not believe you. But either way, they won't care, so save your energy for fetching them a biscuit.

5. Apologising for your home serves to draw your guests' attention to your mess. It is far better, instead, to distract your visitors from their surroundings. Tell a joke. Do a twirl.

Pull a rabbit out of your ear! Light a fire in the kitchen! Wave a packet of chocolate biscuits in their face! With the right diversion, your guests will never even notice the mess.

Editor's note: We at HarperCollins strongly recommend against lighting a fire in a kitchen.

You need never apologise for being an actual human person who lives in an actual lived-in home. Having said that, an apology is occasionally warranted, and I have outlined the circumstances below.

Eleven reasons why you should apologise to your guest

1. You have no coffee in your house.
2. You have no chocolate biscuits in your house.
3. You have no toilet paper in your bathroom.
   (I once visited the home of a male friend and discovered the absence of toilet paper a fraction too late. It created quite the predicament, and I would urge you to ensure that your bathroom is always fully stocked.)
4. Your home smells like lamb casserole and it's ten in the morning and your guest is vegan.
5. Your rabid dog attacks your guest.

6. Your perfectly nice dog eats your guest's handbag. (This happened to me when I was at a friend's home for dinner. I'm not saying that I now dislike the dog, but my affection for it has definitely cooled.)

7. A painting falls off your wall and knocks your visitor unconscious.

8. You welcome a guest into your home and (surprise!) their despised ex is in the living room drinking tea.

9. You accidentally open your front door to a visitor with one of your breasts hanging out. (I did this once when I was breastfeeding my first child and the postman looked quite unsettled.)

10. You accidentally serve your dinner guests a slightly undercooked chicken and unwittingly put them at risk of salmonella poisoning. (What can I say? I am an aspirational home-management influencer, not a chef.)

11. You invite an attractive friend over for a romantic evening and he turns out to be violently and terrifyingly allergic to your cat. (This may or may not have happened to me, and it was definitely not romantic.)

But never, ever apologise for your mess. Try this instead: 'Hello! It's so great to see you! Come in and sit down. How many chocolate biscuits would you like?'

Likely Consequences of Your Mess

□ NOTHING AT ALL ■ SOMETHING CATASTROPHIC

THREE

Every mess has a silver lining: the rewards of imperfection

The cup is already dirty

Mess, for the tidy person, evokes a deep sense of frustration. The tidy person mops and sweeps and wipes and dusts, yet within hours, or even minutes, the house is messy again. They long for the satisfaction of a perfectly ordered home, but are constantly thwarted in their efforts by the presence of other humans.

Tidy people believe that their lives would be easier if only their house didn't keep getting so messy. Specifically, tidy people believe that their lives would be easier if only people didn't keep making so much mess. More specifically, tidy people believe that their lives would be easier if only 'Adam, with his filthy shoes' and 'Sarah, who wouldn't notice a wet towel if it jumped up and bit her' and 'Leo and his bloody midnight snacks' would just clean up after themselves.

This relentless frustration and resentment isn't good for their health. Tidy people experience stress and anxiety, sigh deeply and slam laundry bins, and ask exasperated questions like, 'Why is there sand all over my clean floor?' and 'Who spilled the milk?' and 'What are these crumbs all over the kitchen?'

But how do tidy people respond to the vexation of mess? What do they do when their cleaning efforts are brutally defiled?

They clean again.

Yes, despite seeing over and over that cleaning can only lead to heartbreak, they grab their buckets and mops and go back to work, tidying up after Adam and Sarah and Leo with bitterness in their hearts and an apron over their clothes.

Tragically, these tidy people have got it the wrong way around. They have hit the target (or at least scrubbed it clean) but missed the mark. You see, it is not the mess that is causing tidy people to become frustrated. What is causing tidy people to become frustrated is the cleaning! Once you end the battle and stop madly tidying up, you instantly banish the aggravation of mess.

Annoyed that your partner traipses through the house

in dirty boots right after you've mopped the floor? Don't mop the floor and the problem is solved!

Enraged to see food smears and crumbs in your clean kitchen? Don't clean the kitchen and you won't notice they're there!

Constantly hanging up towels that have been dropped on the floor? Leave the towels where you find them and your sanity will be saved!

Buddhist teacher Ajahn Chah once wrote, 'To me this cup is already dirty. Because I know its fate, I can enjoy it fully here and now.' His lesson is this: when you accept that your cup will eventually be dirty, you can stop worrying about whether it is perfectly clean and enjoy drinking your tea. When you can understand that your home will soon be wrecked, you can stop fighting the mess, and take a nap.

> **Editor's note:** What Ajahn Chah actually said was, 'This cup is already broken.' We apologise to the reader for this bastardisation of a sacred text.

A biological purpose

There are many excellent reasons to embrace the joy of mess, whether or not you have children. But if you *do* have children, it seems absurd not to.

For a start, you will have very little choice in the matter. From the moment your baby is born, you will be surrounded by mess. Children generate mess like the sun generates heat, or influencers generate inspirational memes. You can spend the next eighteen to twenty years trying to rein it in, or you can relax and just go with the flow.

More importantly, mess helps your kids in their journeys towards becoming self-actualised adults. Now, there is a terrible misconception in our modern society that caregivers should teach kids to be neat and tidy. This is a myth born of cleaning blogs, parent forums and Super Nannies, along with the manufacturers of trundle beds and 'teen wardrobe solutions'.

But there is no need for kids to be scrupulously neat, other than to appease their mess–averse parents. Kids need mess like adults need coffee, paracetamol and wine; it keeps them operating at their full potential and wards off despair. Mess is in a child's DNA, and in their grotty little soul. Kids are genetically programmed to wreck their immediate surroundings, and need to fulfil this biological purpose in order to grow and develop.

Babies

Babies are the purest manifestation of mess. You put food in one end and mess comes out the other. But that's not all! Dribble, tears and vomit come out the first end too, so it's really just mess every which way. Literally all babies do is create mess and offer the occasional toothless smile. It is their sole function in life for several months, until they add other activities to their repertoire, such as learning how to locate their hands and trying to chew on their own toes.

Toddlers

As babies develop into toddlers, they pass an important developmental milestone: they gain the ability to generate mess using external sources as well as their own bodies. Toddlers learn about their environments by banging, scratching, smearing or spattering anything that isn't nailed down. This exploration of the physical world should not be stymied in any way. If a toddler can't pour liquid soap onto the carpet, or knock a hole in your wall with the meat tenderiser, or rub Vegemite all over their baby sister, how can they discover what it means to be human?

Older children

Kids from around five to twelve years of age offer their caregivers a temporary reprieve from the endless tsunami of mess. This is not because they suddenly become considerate, or develop a passion for the aesthetics of #homeinspo; rather, this is the age at which kids discover screens. They will of course break things with soccer balls, spill Lego on the floor and drip nail polish and/or slime onto your shagpile rug. Still, you will have blessed relief when they spend hours learning TikTok dances, binge on movies about superheroes and watch YouTubers do weird things with food.

Teens

As a child morphs into a teen, they embrace mess as a lifestyle and a religion. Rubbish is flung in the vague vicinity of a bin. Wardrobes are forgone in favour of floordrobes and chairs. Bathrooms overflow with bottles of mysterious liquids, various aerosol sprays and used cotton balls. Bedrooms become repositories for all manner of horrors: leftover foodstuffs, crumpled tissues, crusty mascaras and festering backpacks. Mess is a way for teens to express themselves, and a way to bug the hell out of their order-obsessed parents. Mess teaches teens how to individuate from their families, and how to locate a clean t-shirt under a mountain of dirty clothes.

Hang on, I'm on the phone …

Living with other people can be infuriating, even for people who aren't averse to mess. Sure, it's very pleasant at family dinners when, miraculously, everyone is in a good mood. And yes, it's lovely to have someone to cuddle up to at night, if they don't hog the blankets or snore.

But the people you live with can also be demanding and selfish and thoughtless and annoying and exasperating and vexatious and loud. They insist that you watch their recorder concert in the living room when you just want to read your book. They eat the leftover spaghetti bolognaise for their breakfast when you have been eagerly saving it for your lunch. They spend an hour in the bathroom, perfecting their winged eyeliner, when you just want to have your shower and go to sleep.

It is hard to live with other people without spending much of your time in a state of subdued aggravation. I adore my kids, but most days are a series of petty irritations punctuated by moments of profound love and joy.

We all must deal with the daily delights and challenges of our family's various personalities: their moodiness, their loud chewing, their complaints of 'there's nothing to eat in this house!', their weird tendency to lie on the floor so you must step over them to get to the kitchen. (I'm assuming that all kids do this? If not, then no, mine don't do it either.) There is enough conflict to manage every day without adding mess to the very long list.

And, if you are concerned about mess, there will certainly be conflict, particularly when you're dealing with kids. Trying to get kids to clean when they don't want to clean is a lot like herding sheep. They will bleat a lot and stop regularly to look at the sky, and you'll need to be on their tails the entire time.

What's more, kids tend to be extremely skilled at deflecting requests to tidy up. If you ask them to do so, you will receive one of a set of stock answers, as listed in this helpful table below:

Parental request	Child's stock response
Why is the microwave covered in slime?	I don't know.
What is that on the carpet?	Nothing.
Why is the mirror covered in toothpaste?	I didn't notice.
Why are there dirty tissues *right next* to the bin?	I missed.
Can you please put my eyeliner back in my drawer?	Hang on, I'm in the middle of a game.
Can you please put the Vegemite back in the pantry?	Hang on, I'm in the middle of an episode.
Can you please hang your towels up on the rack?	Hang on, I'm on the phone.
Can you please put your shoes back in your room?	Hang on, I'm doing homework.*
Can you please empty the dishwasher?	It's not my turn.**
Can you please clear the table?	Why should *I* do it?
Can you please put the cereal back in the pantry?	But Jack took it out!***

* Lies, she is on the phone.
** Lies, it totally is her turn.
*** True, he did, but she ate the cereal too.

Fortunately, convincing an adult to do their fair share of the housework is much easier than it is to convince a kid.

Oops, sorry! Auto-correct mistake! Damn computer. What I meant to write was 'is even harder'. To illustrate the difficulty of getting adults to pull their weight, please consider this second helpful table:

Tidy adult's request	Messy adult's stock response
Can you please clean the bathroom?	Yeah, I'll do it later.
Seriously, can you please clean the bathroom?	I told you, I'll do it later!
When are you going to clean the bathroom?	Please don't nag me.
Are you ever going to clean the bathroom?	Oh my God, can you stop nagging me?
For God's sake, can you clean the bloody bathroom?	Nah, I looked and it's fine.

When you stop trying to impose neatness and order in your home, you can reduce the amount of conflict in your household by a factor of one hundred thousand. (This is not an accurate figure, I just made it up, but I feel I have made my point.)

Embracing the magic of mess has saved me and my family a huge amount of angst. Sure, I enforce basic standards – my kids need to be hygienic, and considerate, and not leave slime where it can get into my hair – but beyond that, I generally let things slide. There are far more pressing issues to debate with my kids, such as the amount of screen time they should have, whether capitalism is a destructive force, and whether the winner of this year's *Masterchef* was actually the best cook.

I also never, *ever* argue about mess with my romantic partner. In further news, I don't have a romantic partner, so this is extremely easy to do.

We all need to choose which battles we wish to fight and which hills we wish to die on. There are so many things to argue about with our families. Is a messy kitchen or a pair of dirty shoes on the floor really worth all that conflict and fuss?

Red wine on a white sofa

Guests can tell when our hosts are obsessive about cleaning. We can feel it in the air, and in the coasters under our drinks. We can sense it as they carefully pass us our glass of red wine, their eyes glancing nervously as our hands meet over a pristine white couch. (Also, the pristine white couch is a dead giveaway.) We intuit it in the way they quickly pick our cake crumbs off the table and whisk our coffee cups away before we've swallowed our last sip.

Their homes are lovely to look at but leave us feeling tense, like those super fancy restaurants with the waiters in black tie who say, 'Very good choice' as we order a plate of venison ravioli with a lemongrass reduction. Personally, I prefer to dine at a nice casual bistro, where I can laugh with the wait staff, order an enormous plate of food and eat my chips with my hands, licking the salt from my fingers. Similarly, I prefer drinking tea with a buddy on a couch surrounded by mess to sipping wine on a white sofa.

Of course, a home doesn't automatically become welcoming just because it is untidy. You can't just scatter dirty plates around and dump your laundry in the hall, then expect guests to start hammering on your door. (I know – I tried this. Absolutely no one showed up.) Still, creating a truly welcoming environment for your visitors does include tolerating a certain amount of disorder.

Having said that, I don't judge people who have super-neat homes; it is not their fault that they are so hopelessly tidy. And I'm still happy to visit my #homeinspo friends, though I probably won't risk drinking red wine.

But my advice to you is that, if you wish to make your friends feel welcome, learn to tolerate a little bit of mess. Stop madly cleaning up before your guests arrive. Stop madly cleaning up at all! Relax, and your visitors will relax with you. Drink red wine on a white sofa, and you will drink alone.

It's not mess, it's inspiration

There is a pervasive and possibly defamatory myth that mess is a sign of laziness. I'm not sure who I can sue about this, but I will head to court when I work it out.

I am messy, but not at all lazy, and I am also highly litigious.

Mess is not indicative of laziness, but it is strongly related to creativity. The detritus of a creative person's home is an important part of their process.

This book exists because I am a messy person. If I had been neat, I would have written a very different book; something like *The Sadness of Mess*, or *How to Win Clean Friends and Tidy People*, or *The Power of Positive Sweeping*, and no one would be interested in that!

More significantly, if I weren't messy, I would have slammed shut the door to the portal of creativity that allows me to write at all. The creative process is, by definition, messy, because creative thinking is messy thinking. It is the opposite of logical thinking, where one idea follows another in a linear and rational way. In the world of logic, one plus one equals two. In the world of creativity, one plus one can equal twelve, or fifty-seven, or a penguin, or a haiku about a dream.

And messy thinking is bolstered by a messy environment. This has been demonstrated in scientific studies, which suggest that a cluttered environment can help to increase creativity. People come up with more creative ideas when they're in an untidy room. Mess is not only good for your health: mess is good for your art.

So why does mess encourage creativity? Well, mess is a juxtaposition of things that are not supposed to be together, like a neon balloon in a bathroom, or a pair of underpants on a table, or a small plastic giraffe in the kitchen sink. (I'm not being poetic; I am actually looking around my house.) And these unexpected juxtapositions encourage us to make similarly unexpected connections between ideas, breaking out of rational and predictable trains of thought.

Mess is, quite literally, inspirational.

If you want to release your creativity, you need to let go of your desire to tidy. Order and neatness encourage a rigidity of thought and don't allow the unexpected and surprising into your life. How can you make great art when constrained by hospital corners on your bed? How can you feel inspired without clutter upon which to gaze? How can you let your creative juices flow without the inspirational incongruence of a small plastic giraffe in your kitchen?

To be creative, you need to be more in your head and less in the bathroom with a mop. You need to focus your energies on honouring your creative process and leave the laundry and the dishes to their prosaic dull fates. You need to ride waves of inspiration across the seas of your imagination and not swim back to shore to sweep the sand from your floors. And you must choose a metaphor considerably more original than the one you just read.

Messy people are creative, and creative people are messy, and one person's mess is another person's inspiration. If you're messy, take note: you are not a lazy person, you do not have low standards, and you do not need to change.

You are riding the waves of your imagination.

> **Editor's note:** To clarify, this book does not exist because the author is a messy person. This book exists because a contract was offered to the wrong writer by a junior editor who is no longer in our employ. Furthermore, we would definitely be interested in *The Sadness of Mess*, *How to Win Clean Friends and Tidy People*, and *The Power of Positive Sweeping*.

Mess is chill

One of the greatest benefits of embracing the joy of mess is that you attain a certain amount of chill. When you learn how to walk past an unmade bed, or to leave a cupboard door open in the kitchen, or to put off dusting for yet another day, you learn how to let things go.

Extremely neat people exert a great deal of energy ensuring that their homes are perfectly in order. They are constantly scanning their environments for things to clean and tidy, even when they're supposed to be relaxing. They might be watching the finale of their favourite Netflix series, or chatting to a friend on the phone, but the sight of a crumb on the floor or a coffee mug in the sink will have them leaping into action like a fireman at an alarm. These poor humans are perpetually on high alert, unable to drop their guard for a minute, even in their own homes.

Extremely neat people say things like:

- 'I can't sit down if the dishes aren't done.'
- 'I can't possibly leave the house without making the bed.'
- 'Open cupboard doors make me anxious.'
- 'Please don't touch the glass balustrade – I just cleaned it!'
- 'Why is that blue book on the red shelf?'
- 'Those shoes don't belong in the hallway!'

We messy people don't have those concerns. We messy people say things like:

- 'This Netflix show is really good. Let's watch another episode!'
- 'I might just have a little nap.'
- 'Ooh, look! I found half a chocolate bar in the couch!'
- 'Reckon I can wear this top a third day in a row?'
- 'Don't worry – it's just a stain!'

- 'Gorgeous shoes over there in the hallway. Are they new?'

When an obsessively neat person sees something out of order – a wet towel on the floor, or grubby finger marks on the wall, or a dirty dish in the sink – their stress response is immediately activated. The towel/finger mark/ dish screams 'DANGER!' (yes, just like that, in big capital letters) and their bodies respond by getting all twitchy and agitated. They cannot relax until they have cleaned it up.

Those of us who are comfortable with mess either don't experience that stress reaction, or have learned how to ignore it. We can notice the finger mark on the wall and decide we'll get to it when we're ready. We don't get irritated by dirty dishes or imperfections, and we don't sweat the small stuff. We just notice the small stuff lying in the middle of the floor and step right over it on our way to make a cup of tea.

Learning to tolerate mess and disorder is an invaluable life skill. Life is random and chaotic, and throws up constant challenges, and we all need to be able to adapt. But how can we manage disappointments and deal with change if we can't even cope with an open cupboard door? How can we learn to roll with the punches if an unmade bed sends us into panic? How can we deal with the vicissitudes of life when we are unsettled by a pile of schoolbags?

If you are extremely neat, I won't tell you to relax. (Honestly, there is nothing more stress-inducing than being told to relax, or – even worse – to 'calm down'. I could be fast asleep in bed and the word 'Relax!' whispered from two rooms away would make me immediately jolt awake and bristle with tension.) But if you *do* wish to relax, start by accepting a little bit of mess. Once you can make peace with a small plastic giraffe in your sink, you can begin to make peace with yourself.

Mess is beautiful

If I wasn't so chill, I would be enraged at the unreasonable and unrealistic beauty standards in the home-management space. We are conditioned to believe that the domestic ideal is a clean, tidy and decluttered house, just as we are conditioned to believe that the female beauty ideal is a small waist, big lips and weird high-waisted jeans that look hideous on anyone over the age of twenty.

But these beauty ideals are just cultural constructions. The whole concept of beauty is entirely subjective, whether we're talking about a home, or a face, or a pair of jeans. One person's beautiful is another person's hideous, which is why my daughter and I are currently deep in disagreement over whether she should pierce her septum.

We need to break free from prescribed beauty standards; in our homes and in life in general. (But not in the septum. That is a separate matter entirely.) We need to broaden our definition of beauty to include a wider range of aesthetics. There is beauty to be found in all sorts of homes, from the pristine to the completely chaotic. We should celebrate untidy homes with the same fervour and joy with which we celebrate the neat.

If a home was a work of art, a neat home would be a carefully constructed line drawing, with sharp edges and straight lines and lots of clean, white space. A messy home would be a Jackson Pollock, all colour and chaos and spatters, with peanut butter rubbed into the centre and a pair of dirty socks at the edge of the canvas. Neat homes are static and unchanging and consistent; messy homes are vivid and constantly being updated. Neat homes are a perfectly serviceable bowl of vanilla ice cream, but messy homes are the full glorious chocolate sundae, with sprinkles and wafers and sauce and cream dripping decadently down the sides.

If a home was an outfit, a neat home would be a business suit, whereas a messy home would be boho chic. What looks like clutter is actually a layering effect that is a deliberate stylistic choice. Just as fashion influencers layer jewellery and pieces of clothing, so we home-management influencers layer items in our homes. My dining table features half an apple on top of a stack of papers on top of a laptop on top of a book, beside a tube of hand cream inside a cracked coffee mug on a plate that is covered in crumbs. The mismatch of different textures and colours creates a fascinating vignette that is extremely on trend, and brings interest and charm to the room.

What's more, the juxtaposition of discordant items in my home creates a powerful fashion statement. My wet towel clashes with the shiny tiled floor to create a fabulously striking bathroom. My neutral couch contrasts with the pile of coloured laundry to really make my lounge room pop. The pink running shoes in the hallway are strikingly incongruous and highlight the rich brownness of the floorboards.

The key elements of any form of artistic expression are confidence and conviction. If Jackson Pollock had apologised sheepishly for his work and explained that he had been trying to paint a neat square, he may never have sold a single painting. You need to stand tall, own your mess, and claim it as the masterpiece that it is. Your home is perfect in its imperfection. It is chic. It is fascinating. It is beauty. It is art.

Procrasticleaning

There are those who clean because they love to clean, and there are those who clean out of a sense of obligation.

But there is a third group of cleaners, driven by less wholesome motivations, who serve neither themselves nor others. A broom is only as virtuous as the hand that pushes it, and some hands are clutching that broom for all the wrong reasons. There is a dark side to cleaning, and I know this because I have ventured there myself.

I embrace mess and I hate cleaning … except when I have a deadline. Suddenly, with work pressures looming, I will feel an overwhelming desire to organise my pantry, or to change all the linen, or to go searching for dust in the corners of the living-room shelves. I will sit down at my computer to do some work, then find myself donning rubber gloves and grabbing the window cleaner. I have committed to finally doing my taxes, only to realise that the floors must be urgently vacuumed. Whenever it is time to send out my invoices, I am driven to clean out the fridge, or steam clean the carpets, or paint the entire house in a new and vibrant colour.

Happily, I send out invoices only every couple of months.

There are times when a clean is just a clean, but there are other times when a clean is a delaying tactic. I recently conducted a wide-ranging survey of seven of my closest friends and discovered that fifty per cent of them clean and tidy to avoid doing something they don't wish to do. (And yes, fifty per cent of seven is three and a half, but we don't need to get pedantic here.) Cleaning is the ultimate procrastination tool and has been abused by dawdlers since the dawn of time. I'm no historian, but I am quite sure that when prehistoric man needed to go out and hunt wild boar, he would suddenly feel an irresistible urge to sweep his cave.

Are you a procrasticleaner? Do you find yourself washing the walls when you're supposed to be reading a report? Do you put off responding to emails in order to reorganise your wardrobe? Do you say things like, 'I'll just quickly polish all the silverware and then I'll make that call'?

When you learn not to use cleaning as a crutch, when you can resist the distracting call of the sponge, your productivity will soar. You will get through your unpleasant jobs more quickly and efficiently and have more free time in which to clean. Except, of course, you won't use your free time to clean; without work to be avoided, you will have no need to procrastinate! You will just relax in your gloriously messy home.

Don't let the dark force of cleaning divert you from your purpose. It's time to put down the broom, let the dust pile up in your cave, and go back to hunting boar.

Cost-benefit analysis

Life is short. It really is. It absolutely whizzes by. Just a minute ago I was a teenager strutting around in a tiny bikini, and now I'm taking pain meds for my back and slathering on wrinkle creams that don't work. How do we want to spend our precious years on Earth before we fly up to the Great

Laundry in the Sky? What percentage of our lives are we prepared to devote to the unwinnable battle with entropy? How much housework do we really want to do?

Is it even worth the effort?

Costs of achieving a perfectly clean house	Benefits of achieving a perfectly clean house
• Enormous amounts of time and energy exerted in a futile and exhausting battle against the Second Law of Thermodynamics (see page 46). • Daily physical contact with gross things like toilets and oven grease and dust balls and decomposing fridge vegetables. • Teeth-clenching frustration at seeing members of your household casually desecrate your pristine floor/kitchen/bathroom/living room just minutes after you've cleaned it. • Unpleasant, recurring arguments with members of your household over their failure to respect the sanctity of your clean floor/kitchen/bathroom/living room. • Overly sanitised environment leading to the degradation of natural immunity (see page 40); also, the pervasive smell of bleach. • Friends being intimidated by the fearsome perfection of your home, leading to awkwardness, tension and fewer dinner invitations. • Procrasticleaning, resulting in missed deadlines and failure to lodge tax returns, causing career decline and possible fines. • Less time to explore other sources of satisfaction that don't involve a sponge or broom.	• Intrinsic satisfaction of having a clean and tidy home for three or four minutes before the mess creeps back in. • Visitors saying, 'Wow, your house is really clean!' • Um … • Give me a sec … • I'm sure I can think of something else! • Nah, that's pretty much it.

Forty-three wonderfully satisfying things to do instead of cleaning your hous.

1. Read a book. Alternatively, write your own book. Not one about the benefits of accepting mess, though – that one is already taken.
2. Make some art. Notice how it imitates life.
3. Learn to meditate and become self-actualised.
4. Search on the internet for an unsolved crime, solve it and then make a podcast about your investigation.
5. Make tiny crocheted lemmings and sell them on Etsy.
6. Watch blooper videos on YouTube and have a good laugh.
7. Watch reunion videos on Instagram and have a good cry.
8. Take up a sport. I haven't done this since I played netball in Year Six but apparently there is a wide and exciting range of sports to try. Luge sounds interesting. So does zorbing. Perhaps give extreme ironing a miss.
9. Start posting some tasteful selfies and become an Instagram influencer.
10. Have a nap. You don't even need a bed! You can nap on the couch, on the floor or under a

tree in the park. I once napped in my car in a supermarket carpark and it was deeply satisfying.

11. Learn a new language – preferably French. Who doesn't want to be able to speak French?

12. Research the share market, open a portfolio and start building a personal fortune.

13. Play with your pet. If you don't have a pet, adopt a pet. May I recommend a cat? They are self-cleaning.

14. Watch that Netflix series that everyone is talking about and then analyse it with your friends. (Personally, I thought the ending was disappointing, but I didn't see the twist coming at all.)

15. Buy some plants and try very hard not to kill them.

16. Learn a musical instrument – the piano or guitar if you prefer something melodic, and the recorder or drums if you hate your family.

17. Start a book club with your friends and talk about pretty much everything other than books.

18. Take an adult dance class. (By this I mean a dance class for adults, not a class in 'adult dance', though I am open-minded and the latter sounds quite exciting.)

19. Study philosophy and figure out the meaning of life. Is it to clean?

20. Start a cult and recruit some followers. Alternatively, start your own multi-level marketing scheme.
21. Look up the Facebook page of someone who bullied you at school and take pleasure in how poorly they are aging.
22. Invent something and get venture capitalists to invest in your start-up.
23. Daydream. Just … daydream. (If you don't know where to start, try fantasising about having a full-time cleaner.)
24. Start a conversation with a stranger. Uber drivers are interesting.
25. Plant some seeds and start a herb garden. Not coriander, of course. Coriander is Satan's weed.
26. Edit a Wikipedia entry. Be creative! Have some fun!
27. Learn witchcraft and start casting spells.
28. Create an online dating profile and start looking for love.
29. Do your taxes. Encourage me to do my taxes. Do my taxes for me.
30. Read a long-form article about something other than the terrible state of the world.
31. Go for a walk. Go for a jog. Do a yoga class. Go to the gym. Do an online exercise class. Become a personal trainer!

32. Have sex with someone who enthusiastically consents to having sex with you. (This person can be yourself.)

33. Go online and do a deep dive on one of your favourite celebrities.

34. Get some therapy. After a few sessions, use all your new insights to become a life coach.

35. Collect something. (I would suggest something other than navel lint, but whatever floats your boat.)

36. Start a journal and write in it every day. In twenty years, you can look back at your entries and laugh in horrified mortification.

37. Build a bunker, stock it with supplies and become a doomsday prepper.

38. Learn to make your own clothes and start a fashion label with a quirky name like Jtebski or Secretion.

39. Dance in your living room like nobody is watching. (If you dance like me, it is probably best if nobody *is* watching.)

40. Send messages to friends using only auto-fill.

41. Browse through online stores, fill up your cart then log out again.

42. Start a YouTube channel and post about the joys of not cleaning.

43. Do absolutely nothing at all.

Conclusive proof that mess is better than cleaning

FOUR

Get stuffed: why you should stop throwing out your things

Keep the cow

Reader:

What I am about to disclose may come as a great shock to you, so I apologise in advance for the distress it may cause. I suggest you sit down, if you are not already seated, and take a moment to summon your resilience.

OK. Here goes. Here is my confession:

I was once an enthusiastic declutterer.

Yes! I know. It is a shock, and upsetting. You probably feel blindsided by my revelation. I apologise – I should have told you earlier, but I feel a great deal of shame about this disturbing phase of my life. Rest assured that it is over and I am now completely cured!

Though it is no defence, it may comfort you to know that I didn't pick up decluttering from a social-media trend. My decluttering phase took place long before the decluttering craze had taken hold. I engaged in the Japanese art of decluttering before the Japanese art of decluttering was a thing. I performed the Swedish art of death cleaning when I was thirty-five and healthy. I spent hours going through my cupboards, culling anything that seemed redundant and experiencing waves of satisfaction as I threw my cast-offs into a charity bin. (Or, at least, as I threw my cast-offs into the car, where they marinated for a month or two before I summoned up the energy to drive to a charity bin and toss them in.)

I did not use the phrase 'spark joy', nor did I thank my items when I threw them away. (Even as a much younger woman, I realised that inanimate objects don't speak English or any other language.) I certainly didn't post my decluttering on social media, or hashtag it with #lessismore, or #nojoyhere, or #simplifyyourlife.

Still, this journey to the dark side did give me first-hand experience of the perils of the decluttering movement. I have lived with sparse wardrobes, meagre toy cupboards, empty bookshelves, minimal accessories and a profound, lingering sense of regret.

So how did this happen? Why did I start throwing out my possessions?

Well, I would declutter whenever I felt stressed or anxious, to regain a sense of control over my life. I would rummage through my home in a state of agitation, looking for superfluous items to discard.

'I haven't worn that blue t-shirt in months!' I'd cry, forgetting that it was winter, and that summer would almost certainly come back around.

'This crockpot is old,' I'd declare, although pots don't have use-by dates, and there was plenty of room in the drawer since I'd thrown a 'spare' saucepan away the week before.

'This papier-mâché cow is ugly,' I'd say, even though I'd bought that cow in Bali on a holiday, and it was as beautiful as any papier-mâché cow I'd ever seen.

'You don't play with this Barbie anymore!' I'd whisper in the dead of night, because my daughter was fast asleep, and if she'd known I was plotting to get rid of her toys – even the ones that had been sitting in the toy cupboard for a year – she would have leaped up and snatched them out of my hands.

I would then shove all the decluttered objects into a garbage bag (or, once, into a suitcase I had decided we didn't need) and take it out to the car. I'd immediately feel lighter as I walked back into the house, partly because of the psychological relief, and partly because the bag of rejects had been extremely heavy.

I would feel good for the rest of the day – sometimes for several days afterwards. But inevitably, a week or a month or more later, I'd remember one of the items I'd impulsively discarded and be hit with wrenching remorse. *That blue t-shirt would be absolutely perfect with this outfit*, I'd think; or, *I could really use that crockpot tonight*.

And God help me when my daughter realised that I had thrown out her Barbie! It hadn't been unwanted, I learned as she shrieked at me. It had simply been 'resting' in the cupboard.

Remorse is the flipside of the decluttering movement, and its legacy lasts longer than the satisfaction of discarding. Now, no one wants to be a hoarder, and I'm not advocating holding on to rubbish, but if you need to meditate on whether something should stay or go, you should probably default to 'stay'.

Here's the thing: just because you haven't used that waffle iron in the past six months doesn't mean you won't ever use it again. Just because you haven't worn hairclips since you cut a fringe doesn't mean you won't grow out your fringe in the future. And just because a papier-mâché cow fails to spark joy on a particular day doesn't mean you won't wake up in the middle of the night a year later and think, *Oh, papier-mâché cow, what did I do?*

Decluttering doesn't consider the seasonal nature of fashion, or your own changing tastes and moods. One minute you're throwing out your high-waisted jeans and hair scrunchies, and the next minute they are both perplexingly back in style. One day you're deciding you'll never wear stilettos again, and the next you're thinking, *Life is short! Wear the heels!*

Here's something else decluttering doesn't consider: the environment and consumer waste. Decluttering is positioned as tremendously virtuous (Minimalism! Pare down to basics! Less is more!) but it doesn't do any good for the world. Decluttering won't rid us of any stuff; at best, it moves stuff to a different location. Sure, some of your things may get repurposed if you hand them over to charity, but most of them will end up in the trash. If you're genuinely committed to becoming a minimalist, there is nothing to be gained by decluttering. It is far better to keep using the things you already own and resolve not to buy any more.

You don't need to throw out the things that bring you joy, and you don't need to throw out the things that don't bring you joy. It is far better to have a home filled with clutter than to live in a vast, empty space filled with regret. Hang on to your t-shirts and your pots and your papier-mâché cows. And if you really want to throw something out, grab your books on decluttering and toss them out instead.

Decluttering regrets

In my decluttering days, I discarded many an item that I later came to passionately miss. Please consider this list, learn from my mistakes, and think twice before throwing away your possessions.

Things I wish I had not thrown out:

- A pair of hot pink thongs that I decided were a bit too … much. Clearly, I was in a very dark place and I shouldn't have been making sartorial decisions. Hot-pink thongs are *never* too much. In fact, they are probably not enough.
- A large tin of canned peaches. No one in our house had eaten canned peaches in years. A couple of days later, I had a mad hankering for canned peaches.
- A SpongeBob SquarePants sandwich press that stamped an impression of SpongeBob SquarePants on cheese toasties but tended to burn the bread. I should have been far more tolerant of SpongeBob's failings. There are days when we all need a little SpongeBob magic.
- Several jewellery pouches that I got rid of literally the day before my daughter asked, 'Mum, do you have any jewellery pouches?'

- A pair of billowy transparent white harem pants that were completely impractical. Honestly, I would kill to have them back.
- A charging cord that had been sitting in a drawer for several months, and — as far as I could tell — served absolutely no purpose. As I later discovered, it charged the digital camera that I hadn't used in years.
- Several very glossy lipsticks that I recklessly discarded when I decided I preferred a matte lip. Glossy lips came back in style the following summer.
- A heap of baby equipment, because I'd had my two children and I wasn't going to have any more. As you may recall, I now have three children.
- A brand-new, very expensive vibrator that was gifted to me. I already had a lovely vibrator and decided I would generously bequeath this new one to a friend. A month or two later, the first vibrator broke. I realise now that two vibrators are infinitely preferable to none.
- A seriously beautiful pale-blue chiffon shirt that I wore to death and decided to retire. It has been a decade. I am now ready to wear it again.

- A box full of Lego, because none of the kids played with Lego anymore. A week later my daughter announced that she really felt like playing with Lego.
- A small papier-mâché cow. This is still a very painful topic and I will not be making any further statement on the matter.

Stuff On Display and Stuff Put Away

Clutter is stuff. Stuff is a collection of things. Things bring colour and life and texture to your home.

Clutter is the difference between a gourmet pizza with the lot and a plain gluten-free crust with no cheese. Clutter is the difference between a Netflix period drama with lots of sex and a one-hour documentary on the tax system. Clutter is the difference between a small papier-mâché cow and a pencil drawing of a square on white paper.

Researchers divide clutter into two scientific categories: Stuff On Display and Stuff Put Away.

Most of my stuff is Stuff On Display. This is partly because I love feasting my eyes on precious mementos from my life, and partly because I can't be bothered to put things away in cupboards or drawers. Every single item that I have accumulated over the years holds a special place in my heart and triggers a specific memory or emotional reaction.

There is my son's artwork from his final year at school, which makes me both burst with pride and remember the horrors of final-year exams. There are a dozen or more pot plants which remind me of life and growth and renewal, and also of the neighbours from whom we stole the cuttings.

There is my daughter's learner driver log-book, which evokes those long, terrifying hours I spent teaching her to drive. There is the mug given to me by a friend with whom I subsequently had a falling out, which makes me ponder the volatile and unpredictable nature of friendship. There is the small yellow Lego cat, which brings to mind the whimsy and magic of life, mostly because I have absolutely no idea how it got into our house.

And there is a beautiful ceramic plate featuring a painting of the sea, which reminds me of my daughter's love and devotion. After I accidentally dropped the plate on the floor and smashed it into pieces, she painstakingly reconstructed it for me. My daughter is great with her hands and the plate is as good as new, other than being lopsided, missing several fragments and featuring three giant cracks filled with silicone glue. Such precious memories!

Interestingly, the #homeinspo influencers don't have a lot to say about Stuff On Display. Perhaps even declutterers enjoy having nice things to look at. Perhaps even minimalists, with their cold, austere hearts, appreciate the aesthetics of a seafood plate patched back together with glue.

It is the Stuff Put Away that has come under the sharpest attack from the #homeinspo industry. We are supposed to clean out our cupboards, cull down our clothing to a capsule wardrobe, sort through our drawers, and hone our stuff to the bare minimum. Any possession that isn't in regular use, any item that does not immediately spark joy in our souls, should be transferred to the tip and permanently wiped from our minds.

It is ironic that I used to declutter my own cupboards and drawers, given my childhood predilection for stuff. As a kid, my favourite place to visit was the home of my grandparents, Ada and Joe. Nanny Ada was the Queen of Stuff Put Away. My grandmother would have scoffed at the idea of decluttering or home organisation; she amassed countless fascinating bits and pieces over her lifetime, and she saw absolutely no reason to throw any of them away.

Ada and Joe had plenty of Stuff On Display, too, but it wasn't as exciting as the stuff in storage. Stuff On Display gives you something to look at during mealtimes, but Stuff Put Away gives you something to find.

My grandmother's cupboards were wonderlands of clutter, and my sister and I were free to rummage through them as we pleased. As a result, we were never bored or restless in her home; there was always a drawer to investigate, always a cabinet to dig through, always a wardrobe to get lost in (or to jump out of and scare your sister). Ada's multiple drawers were filled with scarves of every colour, piles of junk jewellery and heaps of tiny, ancient purses. Her bathroom was packed with wrapped soaps, perfume bottles and cosmetics that were considerably older than me. Her wardrobe doors opened to fur coats that smelled of mould, rows of shoes, floor-length frocks and bras with cups the size of my head.

The treasures we found in Nanny Ada's cupboards formed the basis of our imaginary games. My sister and I would dress up in Ada's decaying high-heeled boots, use packs of her old playing cards as currency, and pretend to eat the ancient wrapped soaps as snacks – which honestly wasn't as weird as it now sounds.

If you hang on to your stuff, you, too, could cultivate a wardrobe that offers the same level of excitement to future generations of children. I'm on my way, though my stuff isn't nearly as glamorous as Ada's. I own no floor-length frocks, or furs, or knee-high boots, only a bunch of cheap t-shirts from ASOS, several tracksuit bottoms and leggings, and a couple of pairs of gumboots. Stashed in my wardrobe there are also a dozen little bottles of shampoo that I've stolen from hotels, some old compression stockings, three incomplete sets of baby teeth, a surprising number of cosmetics bags, and five or six pairs of sunglasses in various stages of disrepair.

Still, stuff is stuff, and it forms the fabric of my life, as your stuff forms the fabric of yours. Embrace your clutter. Embrace the joy of stuff. One day, your house might become somebody's favourite place in the world.

Editor's note: Our fact-checker has been unable to locate any research on Stuff On Display or Stuff Put Away, and they do not appear to be genuine scientific categories.

#StandUpForStuff

Before you #getorganised, remember this:

- It is far better to keep things for 'just in case' than to throw them out and buy them again later. Life is long, and endlessly surprising, and you never know when you might need a rubber banana, or a pair of purple leggings, or seven different cosmetics bags.
- Cluttered homes are exciting! For example, if you stick your hand down the back of the couch, you will inevitably come up with a surprise. A scrunchie, perhaps, or a key, or a half-eaten muesli bar, or a small cosmetics bag.
- In the unlikely event of a robber breaking into

your home, you will have plenty of vases on hand to use as weapons.

- A child's cluttered bedroom offers plenty of material with which to create a fascinating obstacle course from door to bed, making bedtime fun for everyone!

- A cluttered floor leaves fewer areas for you to vacuum, thus saving you precious time in your cleaning routine.

- When your kid needs to dress up for Book Day or Halloween, you can create myriad costumes from the assorted stuff around your house. If you're a dedicated clutterer, you'll easily be able to dig up a fake beard, fairy wings, or a sword.

- Your pets will be ecstatic. There is always something to play with in a cluttered home, and always something delightful to chew.

- Cluttered homes are great for scavenger hunts. You could forage for items such as 'a green pen', 'three small tubes of moisturiser', 'a pink crocheted pig' and 'a mug with a logo from a company nobody has ever heard of', and they will all be easily found.

- When a child needs a few coins for school lunch, you can source some from under the couch cushions and the bottom of your wardrobe.

- One day you will invite your wealthy neighbour over for a cup of tea, and she will say, 'I've always loved sherry', and you will pull out that bottle of dusty sherry that has been sitting in your cupboard for fifteen years, and your neighbour will be delighted and put you in her will.
- When your child asks you if you have any tiny spoons/coin purses/spare lipsticks/Lego cats, you will always be able to answer, 'Yes! Yes, I do!'
- You never need to buy pyjamas, because you will have a wardrobe full of old t-shirts that you no longer wear in public.
- You will always have a matching cord for any random appliance.
- When Armageddon occurs (or, you know, there's a catastrophic global pandemic) you will already have seventy-five cans of tinned goods in your pantry. Many will be expired, but when Armageddon occurs (or a catastrophic global pandemic) you can safely eat expired soup. You will also have packets of Dora the Explorer Band-Aids, a variety of medications, plenty of coins that can be bartered for goods, vases that can be used as weapons, old plates that can be used as shields and, possibly, a sword.

FIVE

It's better to be messy than sorry: the perils of home organisation

Mess is in the eye of the beholder

There is a myth propagated by Big Cleaning (or, more specifically, Big Home Organisation, or, even more specifically, Big Declutter) that a messy home must be disorganised, and that the messy person who lives inside it must be terribly inefficient.

Well, I live in a messy house, and I am not inefficient at all. In fact, my mess is a highly sophisticated and effective organisational system, with its own internal logic and order. It might look like chaos to an outsider, but it makes perfect sense to me. Everything is in its rightful place, even if that place is somewhat unconventional and quirky.

The glue, for example, is in the top blue drawer under the envelopes; the iron is in the art cupboard next to the paints; the ironing board is behind the blue drawers containing the glue; my nail scissors are in the drawer next to my bed; the tinned tuna is behind the juice in the pantry; the unopened mail is on a table in the hall. My glasses are on the hall stand, the remote control is on the couch, and if anyone ever feels the need for a yellow Lego cat, it is on the patched-together seafood plate on the dining-room table.

Mess is in the eye of the beholder, not in the pile of papers in the hall.

The #getorganised people would have me rearrange all my possessions to make them more predictably ordered and more conventionally located. Presumably, the ironing board should be next to the iron, the tinned tuna should be next to the tinned salmon, and the mail should be opened and filed away.

But why? My system is bespoke, and it works for me. So what if it takes me an extra minute to locate a can of baked beans? So what if I have to walk five extra steps to retrieve the vacuum cleaner once a month? Who cares if I occasionally pay my bills twice, and occasionally don't pay them at all? I want my home to reflect the vast and fascinating meanderings of my own mind, not the rigid, prosaic systems of an #organisedhome influencer.

There are home-organisation 'solutions' for every corner of your house. If there is a filing cabinet in your office, you can be advised on how to arrange it. If there is a wardrobe in a bedroom, you can be taught to colour-code it. If there is a pantry in your kitchen, you can be shown how to stack the goods in it – and obtain a convenient range of white wicker baskets and labelled Mason jars at a discounted price when you purchase the full, patented set.

But there are perils to these home-organisation systems. Firstly, our brains all work in different ways, and a system that feels deeply intuitive to an influencer might be completely counterintuitive to you. For example, a professional organiser might encourage you to store your cosmetics neatly in a Magic 360° Rotating Cosmetics Shelf™, while you feel far more efficient with your makeup strewn all over your dresser where you can easily grab your lipstick and then throw it back when you're done.

Secondly, a great deal of home organisation is just putting things away when you will only need to take them out again, which is a complete waste of your valuable time. I mean, why should you spend three minutes folding your fitted sheets into perfect squares to store tidily in the linen closet when you're just going to pull them out and unfold them again to make the bed? Why do you need to put the

Vegemite back in the pantry after breakfast when you're just going to need it again for lunch? And why should you open your electricity bill at all when you'll get an alert on your phone when it's almost overdue?

Don't try to squeeze the square peg of your mess into the tidy round hole some influencer is trying to sell you. Be true to yourself and your own bespoke home-organisation system. The tuna can go wherever the hell you like.

Capsule wardrobes are the enemy of joy

Home organisers love the idea of a capsule wardrobe. A capsule wardrobe is a small collection of clothes, shoes and accessories that you mix and match to create a finite number of outfits. A capsule wardrobe is based on classic staples and neutral colours, with a few statement pieces to add interest. A capsule wardrobe is highly efficient and functional.

A capsule wardrobe is the enemy of joy.

My Nanny Ada would have been appalled by the concept. The only capsules she owned were the kind you took with a glass of water when your husband stressed you out and you wanted a good night's sleep. Ada believed that wardrobes should be places of discovery and delight. When she foraged in her wardrobe for something to wear, she could come up with all manner of different

112

looks. She might have emerged wearing a frilled long-sleeved blouse paired with dark-grey pants, or a bright-pink sundress teamed with a wide-brimmed hat. She might have donned a pale-pink velour tracksuit, or a long polka-dot skirt worn with a huge red belt. Getting dressed in the morning was fun for my grandmother, so long as my grandfather wasn't stressing her out and she'd slept well the night before.

My own wardrobe isn't as overflowing with wonder as my late grandmother's. I spent too many years decluttering transparent harem pants to have a comprehensive collection of wonders. Still, my closet is quite chaotic and unruly, and that's exactly how I like it. Frankly, even the *idea* of wearing neutral basics every day makes me feel vaguely depressed. Sure, I might wear the same pair of pink tracksuit pants for an entire week, but I want a range of other options in my closet just in case.

As for wardrobe organisation – well, I reject that concept too. I don't want my clothes all neatly laid out before me, with the jeans on the left and the t-shirts on the right. I don't want my clothes colour-coded and sorted and perfectly hung, so that I can see exactly what I own every time I open the door. I want my jumpers to get lost in the back of my closet, and my t-shirts to get hidden under piles of pants. I want a jumble of clothing and a mélange of shoes, and a mystery box of accessories.

I want to feel a slight frisson when I open my closet doors, and to be able to rummage through my wardrobe and experience the thrill of discovery.

'I'd forgotten about this "Boo Bees" t-shirt!' I'll exclaim, holding the top against my chest as my daughters exchange horrified looks.

'I haven't worn these overalls in years!' I'll cry, knowing deep down that I will wear them again, realise once more that they make me look like a farmer, and retire them for another decade.

'I remember these shoes!' I'll shout. I'll put them on and trot around all day in platform rainbow sandals that I bought on a whim on a holiday, and that feel right approximately once a year.

Clothes are far more alluring when unearthed unexpectedly than they are when hanging in plain sight. An efficient wardrobe might save you time, but a messy wardrobe will be a treasure trove of delight.

Timeline: organising the wardrobe

4.20 pm: Arrive home with a new shirt. It was a bargain! I am delighted with my purchase.

4.25 pm: Shove my shirt in my wardrobe between a puffer jacket and a cardigan. My clothes are a chaotic mess. Shirts are hanging inside out. Jackets are crumpled on hangers. A haphazard pile of t-shirts is teetering on a shelf. A pair of tracksuit pants lies on the cupboard floor next to some tights and a single shoe.

4.30 pm: Gaze at my clothes and then glance at the time. An hour before I need to start preparing dinner. Decide to give the wardrobe a quick tidy.

4.40 pm: Throw my pile of t-shirts on the bed and transfer them jauntily onto hangers like a chirpy sales assistant at Zara. Pause to consider one pale-blue t-shirt that I haven't worn in six months. Decide I will never wear it again and toss it gaily onto the floor, swelling with minimalist pride. I am decluttering my closet down to the basics! Who said capsule wardrobes weren't a good idea?

5.02 pm: Move on to my pants. Pull them all out of my wardrobe and throw them onto the bed, along with a couple of jackets that have somehow migrated to the pants section of my closet.

5.11 pm: Stand back to survey the room. Wow. There are a lot of clothes piled up on the bed. Beginning to wish I hadn't started this.

5.22 pm: Finish hanging the pants neatly onto hangers and begin rehanging the jackets. Realise I am short one coat hanger, which is a problem. Solve this problem by deciding my denim jacket no longer suits me. Throw it on the charity pile and use the hanger for my raincoat.

5.32 pm: My pants, jackets and t-shirts are hanging beautifully in the wardrobe. My jumpers, shirts, undies and pyjamas are still a total mess. I have come this far; I should finish the job. Pull all the remaining clothes out onto the floor.

5.33 pm: Oh my God, what have I done? I am knee-deep in clothes! Feel a sudden wave of bone-crushing exhaustion. I don't want to do this anymore.

5.44 pm: 'Mum, when is dinner?' my son calls.

Look at the mountain of clothes waiting to be put away. 'Soon!' I yell back. Dinner will *not* be soon.

6.01 pm: Have managed to place almost half my clothes back neatly in the wardrobe. In other news, I hate my clothes. I also hate my shoes, my bedroom and this entire day, as well as hating myself for ever opening the wardrobe.

6.20 pm: 'Mum, I'm really hungry,' my daughter calls. 'Can we have dinner soon?'

'Just a minute!' I yell back. Dinner will *not* be in a minute.

6.40 pm: Throwing items of clothing back in my wardrobe with reckless abandon. Anything that I haven't worn in the past few months gets tossed on the scrap heap without a second thought. I discard a pair of navy sandals, a long-sleeved purple top, some pale-grey leggings and a fluffy pink jumper. I am decluttering! I am minimising! I am creating a capsule wardrobe! I am throwing away clothes so I don't need to hang them up!

6.52 pm: 'Mum, I'm dying of starvation!' my daughter wails. Shove the last pile of clothing into the bottom of my wardrobe and firmly shut the door.

6.57 pm: The kids are looking peaky. 'We'll get Uber Eats,' I say.

Next day, 9.15 am: Take the reject clothing to the charity bin. Feel virtuous and proud. There are some nice clothes in there! Some lucky person is going to love them!

Two days later, 8.00 am: Chilly. Look for my fluffy pink jumper. I haven't worn it in ages!

8.07 am: Remember that I have thrown out my fluffy pink jumper. Feel profound regret. Maybe I can wear my denim jacket instead?

8.12 am: Remember that I have also thrown out my lovely denim jacket. Shake my head at my own stupidity and grab a hoodie from the floor of my wardrobe.

Two weeks later, 11.13 am: Buy a new denim jacket.

A pantry paints a thousand words

Despite my flourishing career as a home-management influencer, I have never seen an aspirational pantry in real life. None of my closest friends have beautifully styled pantries, presumably because they are too busy working on their careers, raising kids and posting memes to our WhatsApp group chat.

It is possible that I have visited a home with an inspiring designer pantry, but I haven't wandered into the kitchen to check. That would be impolite, like sneaking into someone's bedroom to inspect their wardrobe, or going into their bathroom and rummaging through their cabinets. (To be fair, I have actually done the latter, but I was looking for some toilet paper at the time.)

I have, however, seen many photos of aspirational pantries, most of them popping up unsolicited on Instagram. Though the styles and the particulars vary, they all look remarkably similar, and they all follow the same governing principle: decant.

Yes, every single item in a designer pantry is decanted. The dry goods are decanted into identical glass jars. The tins and small packets are decanted into large wicker baskets, or – in a modern pantry – large, clear plastic tubs. Even spices are decanted into their own special spice jars, even though *spices are already sold in jars.*

Since the jars and baskets and tubs are identical, they are distinguished from each other by descriptive labels. These labels are written in classic black or white calligraphy on a contrasting background. The sugar is labelled Sugar. The biscuits are labelled *Biscuits.* The Craisins are labelled *Craisins.* The flour is labelled *Flour (Self-Raising), Flour (Plain)* and *Flour (Gluten-Free).* (Every aspirational pantry contains gluten-free options, as well as dairy-free, sugar-free, nut-free and vegan.) The uniform glass jars and white wicker baskets are lined up neatly in their rows, labels facing the front.

These pantries look fabulously organised and wonderfully elegant, but as I peruse the #pantrygoals photos on Instagram, I have many pressing questions about their function.

For a start, pantry organisation is an extremely labour-intensive job for such a private area of your home. A pantry is a storage area for your baked beans and tuna and pasta spirals and jam. It isn't a living room, or a guest bathroom, or even a background for your Zoom calls (unless, of course, you're giving an interview about your pantry). It is one thing to lovingly spruce up a room that is on regular public display. It is quite another to give an extreme makeover to an area that very few people see. Having a designer pantry is a bit like waxing your bikini line when you're single and locked down during a pandemic. Why on Earth does a nook that is hidden away need to be so ruthlessly styled?

Secondly, why are aspirational pantry designers so obsessed with decanting? What is this fear of original packaging? Does a chocolate biscuit taste better when it has been removed from its packet and transferred to a glass jar before it is taken out and eaten? Or is the whole decanting gig just a ruse to allow pantry owners to buy generic biscuits and pass them off as top-shelf brands?

And how do the designer pantry owners manage all this obsessive decanting? Surely it makes life much more difficult and complex? In addition to unpacking the weekly groceries, they must add 'decanting the foodstuffs' and 'lining up the containers' to their list of household chores. I find it exhausting just to bring my groceries in from the car, throw them in the pantry and slam the door firmly. If I had to pour the cocoa into its special *Cocoa* container or tip each packet of Craisins into a dedicated *Craisins* jar, I might give up shopping entirely.

What's more, the logistics of keeping the jars topped up seem extremely complicated and fraught. Take flour, for example (self-raising, plain or gluten-free). Do the pantry owners wait until each jar is completely empty before opening a new packet of flour and tipping it in? Or do they keep topping up the jar of flour, leaving the old, unused flour to languish eternally at the bottom? Is there a crusty inch of decade-old, weevil-infused flour at the base of each beautifully labelled jar?

How do they remember the use-by date of each lot of flour once they've thrown out the original packaging? And is there a separate shelf for all the food in reserve that hasn't yet been decanted into jars? Is there a separate pantry? Is there a storage unit in the garage? Is there a separate room in the house?

Thirdly (or fourthly? or fifthly? I've lost track of the questions), how user-friendly is a designer pantry? Do all those rows of identical glass jars and wicker baskets make specific items easier to find? When I'm looking for chocolate biscuits, I scan the items in my pantry until I land on the packet featuring the photo of chocolate biscuits. This photo helpfully indicates to me that the packet contains chocolate biscuits and not, say, gluten-free flour. Is it really more efficient to scan twenty-seven identical jars for the one labelled *Chocolate Biscuits*? I think not!

Besides, a highly ordered and systematised pantry goes against our basic instincts as humans. We are, as a species, hunter-gathers by nature; we are not supposed to reach out our hands and land immediately on a snack. We are supposed to scavenge a bit, do the work, go on a hunt and rummage around for what we need.

When I want a biscuit, I must dig around in my pantry, towards the back, under the cat food, behind the kilo box of pasta, next to the surprise packet of jelly snakes I'd forgotten I'd bought. My quest to find that packet of biscuits is challenging, but ultimately satisfying, and allows me to feel that I've earned my treat. It is natural. It is intuitive. It is the true gift of the disorganised pantry.

Of course, there's nothing wrong with wanting to have an aspirational pantry. Pantries are extremely important because they contain food. Food is extremely important because it is delicious, and because without it we would be very hungry. But what makes a pantry inspiring isn't how beautifully it's styled. You can't eat a wicker basket or drink a calligraphic label, no matter how gorgeous the font. And you can have the most expensive and perfectly ordered pantry in the world, but if all it contains is lentils, rice crackers and quinoa, then it will be a sad little storage unit indeed.

There is one way to create an aspirational pantry that your family and friends will admire, and you will certainly never need to decant. You need to go to the supermarket and the bottle shop and stock up on the right ingredients.

Ingredients for an aspirational pantry:

- Cadbury Dairy Milk chocolate
- Darrell Lea dark chocolate bullets
- Tim Tams
- Natural Confectionary Company jelly snakes
- Kellogg's Corn Flakes
- Nutella
- Smith's Original chips.
- Black olives
- Crunchy peanut butter
- Ice Magic (for the ice cream in the freezer)
- Crackers (for the cheese in the fridge)
- Really good coffee (for the coffee machine)
- Black tea
- Vanilla Coke No Sugar
- Case of mixed wine
- Gin

- Tonic (for the gin)
- Wicker basket (Ha! Only joking)

Timeline: cleaning the pantry

9.12 am: Look at my diary. Have some work due by close of business. Sit down at the kitchen table with my computer, open a Word document and stare at the screen.

9.20 am: Glance at the pantry. The door is open. Can see that the pantry is a mess. This is no surprise. The pantry is always a mess. Get up to close the pantry door.

9.21 am: Approaching the pantry, notice some crumbs on the second shelf. Again, this is no surprise. There are often crumbs on the shelf. This is a pantry. It contains things with crumbs. Close the door.

9.25 am: Sitting at my computer. Cannot concentrate. This work is extremely tedious. And besides, there are crumbs in my pantry. How can I work with crumbs in my pantry? Decide to get up and quickly brush them away. Then I will be able to focus.

9.43 am: Wiping away crumbs. Moving from shelf to shelf with calm resolve. Smile wryly at a small pile of crushed Corn Flakes as I sweep them into my hand. All is going well. Soon I will get back to work with a nice clean pantry.

9.50 am: Notice a crusty tin of creamed corn. Why would I have bought creamed corn? No one likes creamed corn. I can see that the corn expired eighteen months ago. Gross! Decide to check the expiration dates of all the tins in my pantry.

10.03 am: Wow, I have a lot of expired food! Briskly sort through the tins and dry goods. Soon I will get back to my work.

10.14 am: Notice something moving at the back of the pantry. It's a moth! Suddenly feel tired. Can I ignore it? Decide to ignore it.

10.15 am: It is not a moth. It is *three* moths and a colony of weevils. I cannot ignore three moths and a colony of weevils. Get out the bug spray.

10.26 am: Have been spraying and wiping for days. I am exhausted. Will this job ever be finished?

10.37 am: Sitting on the floor. The entire contents of my pantry are on the kitchen table. Struggle to muster the energy to put them back. I need to work. My deadline is fast approaching. Why did I start this? I need a nap. Who cares about a stupid pantry anyway?

10.40 am: This is ridiculous. I'm going to miss my deadline! Forget neatness. Forget order. Shove all the items randomly back in the pantry. I will organise them later.

10.55 am: Working at the kitchen table. Trying not to think about the unfinished pantry.

11.15 am: My daughter wanders into the kitchen and opens the pantry. 'Wow, this pantry is a mess,' she says.

'Yes,' I mutter. 'I should clean it up.'

Shut my computer and go take a nap.

The home office and the devil's waste

There is an entire subcategory of the home-organisation genre devoted to the home-office desk. (And since a certain recent global pandemic, a lot of people have been sitting at a lot of home-office desks.)

It is no longer enough simply to produce good work at home; you need to produce your good work on an aspirational desk. Your space needs to be perfectly neat and beautifully arranged, adorned with a pot plant in one corner and furnished with sticky notes, coloured markers, pen holders and fancy folders from specialist stationery stores.

Why? Well, according to the #deskgoals people, we need a tidy desk to be able to work at our full capacity. A messy desk, they argue passionately, is a sign of a messy mind.

Now, I could argue persuasively – and I have – that this isn't true. I could argue that a messy desk is, in fact, the sign of a *productive* mind – a mind attached to a person who is far too busy and efficient to sort paperwork into neat piles.

But instead, I shall ask: If this is, indeed, true, what is wrong with a messy mind?

A messy mind is creative. A messy mind is full of thoughts! A messy mind can gaze upon a yoghurt tub, segue seamlessly into the memory of a horror film about centipedes, move on quickly to wonder whether the cat has been wormed, and then cycle back to contemplating what to have for dinner. A messy mind is an infinite portal of ideas. If a messy desk is a sign of a messy mind, then get messy, I say. Pile your desk with detritus and strap in for the ride.

Now, there are a lot of different items that can mess up a desk. There are pens, paper clips, coffee cups, small plastic giraffes and all manner of books. And while the #deskinspo organisers want *all* these items to be in their rightful place, they are particularly fascinated with how to arrange the humble piece of paper.

Yes, within the subcategory of desk organisation is the even subber sub-subcategory of aspirational filing. This is a particularly niche field that focuses exclusively on getting bits of paper off your desk. (Or, in my case, off the hall table, the dining table, the kitchen benches, my bedside drawers and the floor.)

Now, I have strong feelings about paperwork. It is truly the devil's waste. Paperwork is a satanic by-product of our modern world, much like plastic bottles, microbeads and nuclear war. But for the passionate home organiser – and, particularly, the #deskinspo influencer – paperwork offers the purest experience of tidying up. After all, clothes exist to be worn, toys exist to be played with, pantry items exist to be eaten, and books exist to impress visitors; paperwork, on the other hand, comes into the world simply to be filed. There is literally nothing else you can do with a piece of paper other than look at it, place it tenderly into a folder, and slide that folder gently into a drawer.

Still, despite the simplicity of paperwork and its – dare I say – excruciating tedium, the home organisers offer a plethora of ways in which to place your pieces of paper into folders. You can file them alphabetically, numerically, by subject, by date, by degree of importance, or by whatever folder is closest to your hand.

Alternatively, you can get really esoteric and use the Tickler 43 file folder system.

Despite its fabulous name, Tickler 43 is not a boy band, or a sex toy, or a turbo mop, or a cult, or a virus that makes you itchy. Tickler 43 is a very famous organisational system for getting your paperwork under control. (To clarify: It is not famous in the sense of Justin Bieber or Princess Di. People don't put posters of Tickler 43 on their walls, or tattoo Tickler 43 on their chests, or write fan fiction about Tickler 43. Still, it is very well known in filing circles, and has its own Wikipedia entry.)

The '43' in Tickler 43 refers to the number of files in the system. There are twelve files that represent each month of the year, and then another thirty-one files for each day of the month. Your paperwork gets slotted into an appropriate file and each file is then slotted into the appropriate month and day. You check the files each morning and move them around as the weeks progress … and honestly, my brain started hurting at this point in the research and I had to take a break and lie down.

Look, I'm sure there are people who have lots of pieces of paper and enjoy shuffling them around into a variety of folders. But for those of us without weird paperwork kinks, the Tickler system is far more work than it is worth. It requires constant maintenance and constant attention, and offers very little in the way of reward. Yes, it might save you five minutes once a year when you're trying to dig up your car rego, but to save those five minutes you'll be spending hours per month moving paperwork from folder to folder.

As a person who thrives with a messy desk (using 'thrive' in the sense of 'gets her work done eventually'), I can assure you that sophisticated filing systems are unnecessary for productivity. (I can also assure you that small plastic giraffes do not impede one's efficiency in the slightest.) A messy desk can have its own internal logic, even if it seems chaotic to an outsider.

My own bespoke filing systems have been carefully honed over years of working from home. I keep my work documents crammed in a manilla folder on my desk, using a method I call 'Big Bulging Folder'. I keep my unopened mail in a pile on the hall table, a method I refer to as 'Resting My Correspondence'. And I keep my personal documents in a drawer in a cabinet, because the drawer was empty and they had to go somewhere. My desk may be messy, but I know where everything is, and I can find anything by rummaging through the papers. The important things are close, the less important things are further away, and the things I don't need are in the drawer.

Of course, it is occasionally tricky if I must locate an old document that has been sitting in the drawer for five years. But how often do I need to locate an old document? (The answer is 'rarely indeed'.) Absolutely everything except my passport is digitised these days, and my passport will turn up any day now. Paperwork exists merely as a backup in case the interweb is disabled and the whole modern world falls apart. And in the unlikely event of a digital apocalypse, I'm not going to be concerned about my documents. I will be hand-knitting jumpers, stockpiling ammunition and growing my own corn in the garden.

You have better things to do than sorting your bills into subfolders, and far better things to do than moving those subfolders into files. Remember that some of the smartest people in the world have very messy desks, and some of the neatest people in the world hate puppies. And yes, I have evidence that this is true, from a study conducted by scientists. I'd show you, but I have misplaced my notes. I'm fairly sure they're somewhere on my desk.

The bag experiment

The home-organisation industry – and, particularly, Big Declutter – aren't content to transform just our homes. They want to get their tidy, minimalist claws into that little piece of home we carry around with us all day: our handbags.

Apparently, even our handbags are supposed to be neatly culled down to the bare essentials. We are to believe that this will save us tons of time and make our lives so much more efficient. Except ... the whole point of a bag is to carry stuff around, and the more stuff you carry, the better. Besides, how much time can it possibly take to find your lipstick or keys in a bag? It's not a library or a train station. It's a pouch you carry over your shoulder.

Even in my wildest and most misguided decluttering days, I would never have dreamed of trying to organise my precious handbag. Even the idea of a spare and spartan handbag is ludicrous. Still, I am nothing if not open-minded, and when I chanced upon an online tutorial called 'How to Organise Your Bag', I decided, for the sake of research, to give it a go.

Editor's note: In fact, the author was asked to undertake a tutorial named 'How to Thoroughly Spring Clean Your Entire Home in Only 100 Hours', but she declined and offered to do this bag organisation experiment instead.

How to organise your bag: a tutorial

Step 1: Take everything out of your bag

I did this. I poured everything out of my bag onto the table. Out spilled all my personal items and cosmetics and cards, as well as the other flotsam accumulated over the past year, plus enough crumbs to feed a family of birds for a week. My once-proud bag looked deflated and sad, like the discarded empty bladder from a cask of wine. I wanted to reassure my bag that it would be full and happy again soon, but I am a woman of sound mind and I do not talk to bags, so instead I just patted it gently and moved on to step two.

Step 2: Look at all your stuff

I looked at all my stuff and, honestly, I just swelled with pride. There was everything I could possibly need while away from my home, and many bonus items that I wouldn't need at all! There were also a couple of delightful surprises that I'd completely forgotten I owned. I felt like a kid unwrapping a chocolate egg and discovering the cute plastic toy inside.

So, what was in my handbag? Well, in addition to the standard-issue bag-appropriate contents such as credit cards, cash, loyalty cards and unpaid parking tickets, there were:

- Feminine hygiene products, for all my feminine hygiene needs.
- Paracetamol and Band-Aids, for medical emergencies.
- Rescue Remedy, for emotional emergencies.
- A muesli bar, for snack emergencies.
- Tweezers, for when I look in my rear-view mirror and realise there is a rogue hair growing on the bridge of my nose.
- Tissues, for those horrific moments in public bathrooms when I realise there's no toilet paper.
- Lipstick, concealer and mascara, for when I'm at the supermarket and spot my ex-boyfriend in the dairy aisle and need to freshen up my look before he notices me and feels triumphant that I've really let myself go since our breakup.
- A pair of sunglasses.
- A pair of reading glasses.
- Two more pairs of reading glasses!
- Several sachets of sugar substitute, for those painful visits to organic cafés that don't believe in artificial sweeteners.
- Several receipts for clothes that I probably shouldn't have bought and may possibly return one day.

- A small, plastic figurine of a man that probably came from inside a chocolate egg.
- Something wrapped and sticky that was probably once a sweet.
- A key to ... somewhere?
- A small tube of vanilla-scented hand cream from a very nice shop.
- An expired bottle of eyedrops.
- A toothpick that has clearly been used more than once.
- A single drop earring.
- A note that was left on my car by a neighbour with the words *nice park idiot dumbface* (substituted nicer words entirely mine).
- Four nail files.
- Several Q-tips, in various states of disrepair.
- Earphones.
- Yet another pair of reading glasses!

Step 3: Remove what you don't need

OK, this step was tricky. What on Earth did I not need? Most of the items were useful, and the ones that weren't useful were meaningful, and the ones that weren't useful or meaningful were entertaining, and the ones that weren't useful or meaningful or entertaining were the expired bottle of eyedrops, the crumbs and one of the three pairs of reading glasses. (I figured it was important to leave at least two in there; carrying only a single pair of reading glasses is unnecessarily risky.)

'Be ruthless,' the video said, so I sighed and took another pass at my bag's contents. I could return the earring to my jewellery box, but what if I lost an earring while I was out and about and needed a spare? I could remove the key, but I had no idea what it opened, so I had no idea when I might need it next. And I could file the receipts, but I really hate filing, so I decided to let them stay, too.

That left the *idiot dumbface* note, but that was too romantic to discard. There was the small, plastic figurine of a man, which made me smile, so I transferred him to our bookshelf, where he seemed quite content. And there was the sticky something which was probably a sweet but I wasn't sure, so I popped into my mouth to confirm. I was right! It actually was a sweet! I should have left it in the bag.

So that was it. I kept all the other items. I did replace the toothpick, though. I suspected it wouldn't survive another run.

Step 4: Arrange the smaller items into categories and place in small pouches

I arranged the smaller items into piles: medical-type items (pills, Q-tips, toothpick, etc.), glasses, makeup, hate mail and miscellaneous, then placed the groups of items into a series of small cosmetics bags. Happily, I had numerous cosmetics bags in my bedroom, since I no longer declutter my accessories.

Step 5: Put everything back in the bag
Hmmm. I don't mean to disrespect the process, but this step seemed kind of obvious.

So, how did I enjoy my newly organised bag?

Well, my neat bag was terribly efficient and functioned brilliantly for a full nine minutes. At the ten-minute mark, I needed to use my lipstick, then threw it back into the body of the bag instead of the cosmetics bag – sorry, *pouch* – where it belonged. I'm a very busy woman! I don't have time to put things in pouches! Within a day or two, all my items were out of their pouches and jumbled together, except for the note calling me an idiot dumbface, which I had no immediate reason to remove.

While I appreciate the theory of the organised bag, there are three reasons why a messy bag is far more satisfying:

1. A neat bag is efficient, but a messy bag is a joyous lucky dip right there under your arm. You might search for your earphones, or a nail file, or your keys, and emerge with a different item altogether. You might discover a wrapped

sweet, or a random piece of jewellery, or even some poetic correspondence from a neighbour. There is always something to eat. There are always precious memories to relive. There are always tools to engage in some personal grooming when you're stuck in a traffic jam in bright sunlight. The thrill of the unexpected find is worth every extra minute that it takes to locate the item you actually need.

2. A neat bag is aspirational, but a messy bag could very well save your life. I've watched enough disaster movies to know that if a sudden cataclysmic event occurs, it will happen when you're on the freeway with only your favourite child and your handbag. Do you want to be caught in the alien invasion or zombie apocalypse with only your mobile phone and your keys? Or do you want to be caught with a month's supply of medication, a variety of foodstuffs, plenty of feminine hygiene products, some Q-tips and a small plastic figurine?

3. A neat bag is a fashion statement, but a messy bag has character. Anyone can put a generic purse and a generic pair of sunglasses into a generic pouch. It takes a true individual to haul around a year-old muesli bar, a random key and an unwearable piece

of jewellery. Do you want your bag to reflect
the restrained aesthetics of an #organisedbag
influencer, or do you want it to reflect the quirky
and unbridled wonder that is you?

A word on messy cars

Cars aren't technically in the home-management space,
so they are not strictly relevant to this narrative. Still, cars
are definitely home-management adjacent (literally, in the
garage), and many car owners are extremely concerned
about the cleanliness and tidiness of their vehicles.

Your car serves two important but distinct purposes.
Firstly, and most obviously, your car is a transportation
device, a tool to get you from A (in my case, my home)
to B (in my case, the supermarket, my daughter's school,
and that boutique two suburbs away that sells the cute
logo t-shirts).

A tool does not need to be clean to be effective. You
don't need to polish your hammer to hit a nail into a
wall, and you don't need to polish your car to get from
your home to the shops. Your car will not go faster if
you've thoroughly vacuumed the interior, and the brakes
will not work better if you've cleared the water bottles
from the floor. (Having said that, the brakes won't work
at all if there's a water bottle stuck under the pedal, but
that's an easy issue to resolve.)

Your journey will not be impacted if your dashboard is smudged, if there's dog hair all over the back seats, or if there's an empty chip packet in the cup holder. (The exception, of course, is if you're very hungry, in which case an empty chip packet can be frustratingly distracting.) Quite frankly, it shouldn't matter what your interiors look like, as you shouldn't be looking at them at all. You should have your eyes on the road, which is why your car has windows, helpfully translucent so that you can see outside. You should be looking at the other cars, and trees, and houses, and pedestrian crossings, and stop signs, and people. You should be looking at the traffic lights, which will be green as you approach, then turn orange the moment you reach the intersection.

The second purpose your vehicle serves is just as important as its capacity to carry you from A to Boutique. Your car is a mobile storage unit, a suitcase on wheels, a cupboard which follows you wherever you go. It can store lots of stuff that you don't want to keep in your home, and all the stuff you may need when you journey out of the house. If your car wasn't supposed to be a mobile storage unit, it wouldn't have a boot, or door pockets, or all that room under the seats! If a car wasn't supposed to be a mobile storage unit, it would be a motorcycle, or a bicycle, or a horse.

To keep stuff out of your car is to deny it its sacred purpose. At the very least, it should contain a bottle of water, a spare pair of sunglasses, a box of tissues, an umbrella, and some hand sanitiser. It should probably contain several reusable shopping bags, a lipstick, some hand cream, a pair of reading glasses, and some emergency snacks. If you're doing it right, there should also be some clothes destined for the charity bin (which need to acclimatise in the car before being ready for their new home), some books that you totally plan to donate to the street library, a pair of old running shoes in case you ever need to get out and run, and a small toy that was once left behind and now permanently resides in the car. (Ours is a small blue felt whale who has lived in the glove box for so long he is now officially known as Car Whale.)

Your car does not need to be decluttered, but does it need to be cleaned? Well, I am no car aficionado – I recognise my friends' cars by their colour, not their make – but I have been told by people with specialised mechanical knowledge that it is, in fact, important to wash your vehicle. And it is here that cars differentiate themselves from houses and really come into their own.

As you have probably guessed, I am not a fan of washing my own car. It is terribly hard work, and I know that the minute I put down my sponge a bird will fly by and poo on the roof, or it will start to torrentially rain. But I don't need to ever wash my own car, because there is a drive-through carwash nearby. And the drive-through carwash is one of the greatest inventions in the history of Big Cleaning.

I love mess, as you know, but I do not like dirt. I hate cleaning, but I enjoy clean things. So I love nothing more than a machine that cleans for me at very little expense. I love my washing machine, which saves me from handwashing my clothes. I adore my dishwasher, which saves me from using paper plates, because I am not going to wash dishes in the sink. And what is a drive-through carwash other than a giant dishwasher in which humans can come along for the ride?

If I could put my home through a drive-through wash, I would do it in a heartbeat. If I could turn on hoses and blast the inside of my living areas, I would do that too. Outsourcing cleaning to a washing machine that allows you to sit and drink coffee as it does all the hard labour is a gift for which I am eternally grateful. If you have a drive-through carwash nearby, enjoy your bounteous good fortune.

And if you don't, perhaps it's time to take the bus.

PART TWO

A GUIDE TO DOMESTIC IMPERFECTION

SIX

To clean or not to clean, that is the question? Or, how much housework should you do?

A bit of mess

As I may have mentioned once or twice before in this book: life is short. Seriously. It is really, really short. It might feel long when you're in an elevator and the doors don't open immediately and for a couple of eternal minutes you think you might be trapped. It might feel long when you're at the dentist and he's got the suction tube in your mouth and your jaw is starting to ache and it feels like you'll be in the chair forever. It might feel long when you're stuck next to a man at a dinner party who is droning on about his cryptocurrency investment and how non-fungible tokens are the way of the future.

But when you get to midlife, and you're Googling 'How to dye grey eyebrows' and 'How much money do I need for retirement?', you become aware that the years pass by in the blink of an eye.

We all have a limited amount of time on this planet, and we need to think carefully about how we wish to spend it. Life is far too short to be spending hours each week buffing scuffs out of the floor and scrubbing the toilet. Doing it all is overrated! It is time to do just *some*.

Of course, if you genuinely love to clean, then you should go forth and clean, and enjoy every moment with your mop. But if you clean to ease anxiety, or out of a sense of obligation, or perhaps to appease the vengeful gods of domestic perfection, then I urge you to rethink. There is no law that says you need to spend half your life cleaning. It is OK to do the bare minimum of housework. You are allowed to leave a bit of a mess.

But how do you decide what is an appropriate 'bit of a mess'? How can you determine what needs cleaning and what you can ignore? When you are a mess-challenged person who is used to striving for perfection, how can you tell when your home is just clean enough?

To answer this question, please refer to my patented Three-Step Housework Categorisation System™ to help you downsize your cleaning practices for good.

Editor's note: Our fact-checker informs us that this system is not, in fact, patented. The author has just inserted a trademark symbol over the word 'system', which is not legally binding.

Step 1: Triage

The first step in moderating your cleaning habits is to impose a triage system for your housework, much like the triage system used in hospital emergency units. I worked in a hospital for several years, so I have insider knowledge of the highly scientific complexities of the hospital triage process.

A nurse assesses each patient and places them into one of three specialised categories: Urgent, Can Wait and Doesn't Need to Be Here at All.

The patients assessed as Urgent are seen immediately by doctors; the patients classified as Can Wait hang out in the waiting area for a while; and the patients classified as Doesn't Need to Be Here at All can sit on the hard plastic chairs for hours, playing on their phones and eating chocolate bars from the vending machine, before a twenty-year-old doctor finally attends to their ingrown toenail.

Similarly, your housework can be categorised into Urgent, Can Wait and Doesn't Need to Be Done at All.

Just like a nurse, you can assess the seriousness of your housework situation by asking a series of targeted questions. Unlike a nurse, you will not need to wear a stethoscope or a badge – unless you especially want to, in which case I endorse your commitment to the process.

> **Editor's note:** Our fact-checker has confirmed that the author did once work in a hospital, but the above is not an accurate description of the triage system used in emergency units.

Step 2: Be selective

Once you have learned to effectively triage your cleaning, and to put off for today what you can do tomorrow, it is time to figure out what household chores can be put off *forever*.

The home-management influencers would have us all believe that a house needs to be immaculate from ceiling to toilet cistern. But chores need to have a meaningful purpose, and a great many chores do not. If a task doesn't directly or indirectly improve the quality of your life, then it is non-essential; it is a waste of your precious time, and it should be taken off your to-do list permanently.

To clean or not to clean, that is the question?

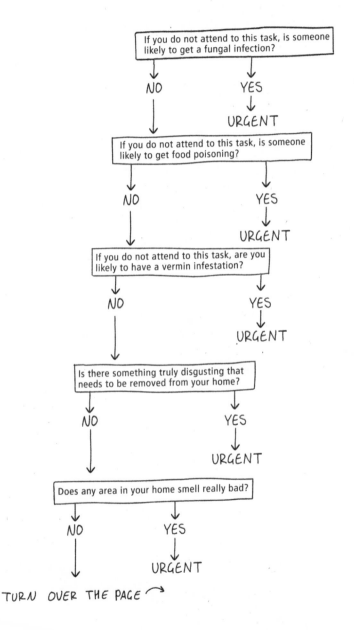

TURN OVER THE PAGE

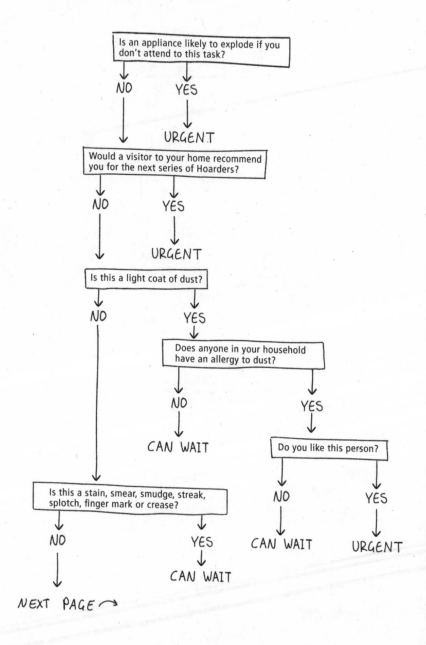

To clean or not to clean, that is the question?

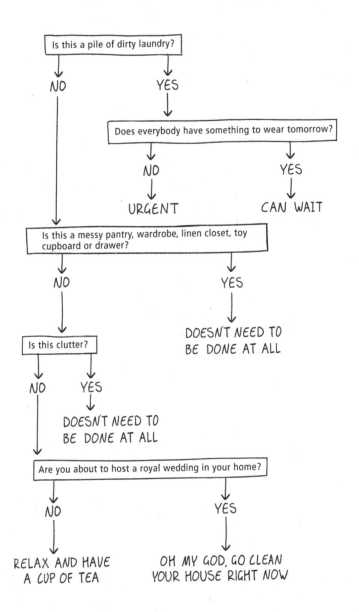

Tasks that don't need to be done at all:

- *Folding your fitted sheets into perfect squares.* This is a cute trick and looks great in TikToks, but it has no practical use whatsoever. No one has ever slept better because their fitted sheet had been folded according to the magical sheet influencer formula. Save yourself the hassle: roll your fitted sheet into a ball and shove it in the linen closet.
- *Ironing your sheets.* See above.
- *Ensuring that your floors are clean enough to eat off.* There is absolutely no need for your floors to be clean enough to eat off, unless you are planning to eat off your floor. And if you are, indeed, planning to eat off your floor, may I suggest that you instead invest in some plates? You can buy them fairly inexpensively and it will save you a great deal of effort.
- *Cleaning anything to hospital-grade hygiene condition.* Your home is not a hospital. There is no need for your surfaces or your utensils or your floors to be sanitised to within an inch of their lives. You are probably not a surgeon, and so you will not be performing surgery anywhere, let alone at home on your kitchen bench using steak knives. And if you are actually a surgeon, I'm sure it was drummed into you in medical school that you

should not do operations in your living room. Clean your home to a moderate degree and leave the sterilisation kit at work.

- *Wiping down your skirting boards.* Literally no one ever looks at skirting boards. They're just there to hold up the walls.

- *Cleaning your light fittings.* If you regularly entertain guests who stand over two metres tall, then there is an argument for cleaning your light fittings. If your guests are of regular height, and you're not living in some sort of subterranean cave with really low ceilings, then no one is going to notice the dust on your light fittings. Leave them alone.

- *Cleaning your small appliances.* Your microwave, your kettle, your Thermomix, and your other small appliances are machines, not pieces of art. You do not need to buff your small appliances to a high shine, or even wipe them down every day. If they are heating up your food, or boiling your water, or whizzing up fantastical meals that could just have easily been prepared without a super-expensive autonomous smart device/cooking companion, then they are functioning perfectly well and need no further intervention.

- *Ironing.* Ironing is perilous. So much can go wrong. On a good day, you can put a crease in the wrong place. On a bad day, you can melt your entire shirt. These days, I won't buy clothes that need ironing; I would rather limit my wardrobe and expand my life. If you must iron, do it carefully, do it on a low heat, do it lightly, and for God's sake don't do it after you've had your evening tipple. Been there, done that. Huge hole in the sleeve.

- *Folding your clothing.* Friends, there is *never* a need to fold an item of clothing. I don't fold anything, ever, and I am a happy and functional person. Folding clothes is tedious and leaves creases in your garments. Placing an item on a hanger is easy and leaves everything looking fresh. I hang absolutely everything except my undies and socks, and those I throw into a drawer. Shelves are bad. Get them out. Put in a rail and get hanging.

- *Folding your recyclable bags.* It pains me deeply to have to point this out, but you do not need to fold your reusable shopping bags. You can shove them in a cupboard, or chuck them in a drawer, or stuff them into another bag, or leave them in the car. It is virtuous enough to try to save the planet. You do not need to save the planet neatly!

- *Cleaning anything that is in a cupboard, in a drawer, under a bed or behind a couch.* There is absolutely no point cleaning anything that isn't visible to the casual observer. Repeat after me: if it can't be seen, it doesn't need to be clean!

Step 3: Clean just enough

The greatest challenge for perfectionists is knowing when to put down the sponge. How do you know when an area of your home is clean *enough*? Sure, it's easy when you're performing a household task that has a clearly defined beginning and end. It is obvious when you have finished emptying the dishwasher, for example, or taken out the trash, or cleared all the plates off the dinner table. (Having said that, this is still a challenging concept for my youngest daughter, who tends to wander off in the middle of completing one of these chores. 'Oh sorry!' she'll say cheerily, when I discover her in her room making slime. 'I thought it was done.')

There are other household tasks, however, that are not so easily resolved. How long do you need to spend cleaning the bathroom, or washing the windows, or mopping the floor? Do you give it a quick once over, or get out the bucket and polish till it gleams? If your housework was a steak, could you learn to serve it rare when you've always cooked it till it's burned?

When it comes to most areas around your home, a cursory clean is all that is required. Save your best efforts for your work, or for your hobby, or for learning to text your group chat and watch reunion videos and listen to a podcast all at once. In most areas of your home, as in most areas of your life, near enough is perfectly good enough.

Tasks that can be done to the least of your ability:

- *Your windows.* Can you see out of your windows? Is it readily apparent whether it is day or night? Will you notice if an asteroid is hurtling through space towards your home? If so, your glass is clean enough.
- *Your floor.* Your floor is a safety feature. Its sole purpose is to prevent you from falling through the ground all the way to the centre of the earth. Your floor does not need to be pristine. It just needs to save you from plunging into a hot molten core.
- *Your walls.* If God had intended for walls to be perfectly clean, he wouldn't have invented art to hang over the dirty spots.
- *Your shower.* Your shower doesn't need to be spotless. Your shower just needs to get *you* spotless.
- *The inside of your pots and pans.* Are your pots and pans hanging on your walls as decoration? If

not, why are you concerned about stains on the inside of your cookware? And if they are on the walls, may I suggest that you take them down and put them back in the drawer where they belong?

- *Your pantry.* There is one clear and tangible way to determine whether your pantry is sufficiently clean: does it have weevils? No? Are there any moths? Also no? Well, congratulations! Your work there is done.

- *Your bookshelves.* In this digital age, actual paperback books are quaint and old-worldly. As such, there is no need to ensure that your bookshelves are completely free of dust, as a fine coating of grime just adds to their retro charm.

- *Your bedroom.* The purpose of your bedroom is to provide a space in which you can sleep. When you are asleep, your eyes are closed. Ergo, your bedroom does not need to be spotlessly clean, because most of the time you will not be able to see it.

- *Your oven.* No one is looking inside your oven, and if they are, it is simply to see whether the rotisserie chicken from down the road is ready to serve. Your oven is not a display cabinet. Your oven is a box that gets hot so that your food can be cooked.

If it is radiating heat and is not at risk of exploding through an excess of oil, then it is acceptably clean.

- *Your laundry.* I don't have a laundry; I have a laundry nook. But really, what is a laundry other than a glorified cupboard that houses your washer and drier? And cupboards, as we have established, do not need to be perfectly clean. If it is messy, close the door and walk away.

SEVEN

If it ain't broke, don't clean it: the cautionary tales

A walk through the roof

My patented three-step system [which is not actually patented –Ed] will work for most tidy people who wish to be liberated from the tyranny of the broom and pan. Still, if you fall on the higher end of the obsessively tidy spectrum, you may need some extra assistance to break free. And so, for you, I will bring out the big guns. I will dig deep and be vulnerable. I will share my personal, deeply traumatic experiences to remind you that cleaning can be a risky business. You can start off with a sponge and the best of intentions, and end up nearly destroying your home and yourself.

My first experience of cleaning gone wrong occurred when I was just nine or ten. I had been quietly reading in my bedroom – probably some story about girls who like horses – when I heard a giant, splintering crash, followed by a man's desperate cry. Terrified, I ran out of my bedroom and past our dining room, where I saw, to my horror, my father's hairy legs dangling from the ceiling. There was plaster dust and shattered fragments of our ceiling everywhere, and, in my panicked confusion, I thought the legs were not attached to the rest of my father's body. This was a gruesome thought, so I screamed, ran back to my bedroom and put a pillow over my head. (This remained my go-to method for dealing with distress right into my teens and twenties.) And there I stayed until my mother, hysterical with laughter, came in to reassure me.

It turned out that my parents, concerned about the state of their rafters, had ventured up into the roof space. Noticing the copious amounts of dust in their hundred-year-old house, my father had decided to give it a clean. Treading carefully along a beam, broom in hand, my dad lost his footing and – as my mother later described it – 'suddenly disappeared'. He fell through the ceiling, where he remained, legs dangling, until my mum managed to hoist him back up.

The good news was that my father's legs were still firmly attached to his body. The bad news was that our dining-room ceiling now needed to be replaced. And those copious amounts of dust, which had been conveniently contained in the roof cavity, were now spread all over the house.

My father should have left well enough alone. It was clear then, and it is clearer now. But I am my father's daughter, and a very slow learner, so I grew up to make my own catastrophic cleaning mistakes, too.

When YouTube killed my oven

A few years ago, I decided to clean my oven. I had read that this was something one should do every few months, so after seven years I was significantly behind schedule. And after twenty billion hot dinners without a clean, my oven was kind of gross.

I used a spray-on oven cleaner, which removed most of the filth, but the door was still caked in grime. I took a closer look and realised that the door was made of not one glass panel but two, and that the greasy detritus of a thousand grilled lamb chops had built up between them.

I figured that I'd need to clean *between* the two glass panels, which would require dismantling the door. I'd need to unscrew the bolts, remove the two planes of glass, polish them up, and put them back together again. It didn't look all that difficult to execute, but neither was grilling a lamb chop and I regularly got that wrong. I realised I would need some assistance.

Sensibly, I called a professional oven cleaner, who came out the next day and did the job.

Oops, sorry! My fingers slipped on the keyboard. What I meant to write was, 'I didn't call a professional oven cleaner. Instead, like a fool, I consulted the internet.'

Yes, I watched a seven-minute YouTube video, which explained to me helpfully that disassembling an oven door is actually extremely simple. You just loosen a few screws, take the door off its hinges and then gently remove the glass panes.

And guess what? The YouTube video was correct! It turns out that it *is* very easy to disassemble an oven door. I quickly dismantled the door and discovered, not two, but three glass planes, as well as a bunch of plastic knobs and a few rubber seals.

I'm a homemaking genius! I thought to myself, as I laid the panes out on the floor and scrubbed them until they gleamed. Who needs a professional oven cleaner when we have the wonders of DIY videos?

After I'd finished the job and stood back to admire my handiwork, it was time to reassemble the oven door. I followed the YouTube instructions in reverse, put the door back together again and stared in satisfaction at my beautiful, clean appliance.

Ha! No, I didn't. If I'd done that, I would be making

my own instructional YouTube videos and raking in the dollars as an #oveninspo influencer.

No, I couldn't work out how to reassemble the glass door. I figured out how to get the glass panes back in the frame, but I had no idea where to place those fiddly little knobs and seals. And this time, the internet was no help at all. Seems there are plenty of YouTube videos telling you how to disassemble an oven, but none telling you what to do when it's in pieces.

I sat there on my kitchen floor, bits of my oven scattered around me, for three long hours. I rewatched the video, and studied the oven manual, but no matter what I did there was always a leftover knob or a rogue length of seal. Finally, as the afternoon turned into evening and my children began asking for dinner, I figured out the solution. I secured the seals over the glass, fitted the knobs firmly in place, and screwed the entire thing back together.

What a thrill! What a relief! I was Queen of the Kitchen! I got out the chops for dinner, switched on my magnificent, clean oven, and plonked down on the couch.

BAM! There was an enormous bang, followed by a shattering of glass, and then an ominous creaking. It was like my father had fallen through the ceiling all over again, except that we lived in an apartment, and my dad was at home with my mum. I ran into my kitchen.

My oven had exploded.

Yes, apparently I had made a teeny, tiny error while reassembling the door. The seals, I learned, had not been in precisely the right place. Who knew a little seal could be so desperately important? My oven was in tatters, along with my ego and, shortly thereafter, my bank account.

It cost me two thousand dollars to buy a new oven, and three days to remove all the bits of glass from my kitchen. It was not quite as expensive as installing a new ceiling, but way more expensive than calling in an oven cleaner.

Two weeks after receiving my brand-new oven, I knocked a tray of hot lamb chops while removing them from the grill. Two rivulets of fat dribbled down the gap in the door, leaving a greasy brown trail between the two glass panes. I looked at the door, sighed, and then looked firmly away.

It was better, I decided, to leave it alone.

A handprint becomes a cloud

I was lying in bed a couple of years ago when I noticed a tiny handprint on my ceiling. It wasn't mine, and it wasn't the cat's, so clearly it belonged to my youngest daughter. Either that or to a demon who haunted my bedroom at night.

Whether human or supernatural, the handprint bothered me enormously. My bedroom ceiling was the last bastion of perfection in my once-pristine apartment. When we first moved in, the place was shiny and new, but after several years it was deteriorating. A bunch of tiles had come loose from the bathroom floor. The snowy-white walls were scuffed and stained. The carpet was fraying where the cat had picked it apart. The cat was looking a bit worse for wear, too.

The polished wooden floorboards were scratched and dented and, in one corner, permanently corroded by acetone. (I had poured nail-polish remover on the floorboards to remove the nail polish I had spilled on the floor, in a modern and equally tragic re-enactment of 'The Old Lady Who Swallowed a Fly'.) The grate had detached from the rangehood above the stove, a downlight had fallen out of its socket and my beautiful new oven had exploded.

But my bedroom ceiling? My bedroom ceiling had been immaculate once, and it would – I promised myself – be immaculate again. I stared in steely resolve at the handprint, then I got out of bed, grabbed a chair from the kitchen, balanced it precariously on my mattress and set to work with soapy water.

The handprint spread. This, in hindsight, was my cue to stop. This was the time to admit defeat and leave well enough alone. But clearly I had learned nothing from the oven debacle, nor had I been sufficiently traumatised by Dad's Ceiling Legs. I continued to clean, with even fiercer resolve. I switched to a spray detergent, and then another. The grime didn't disappear, but moved outwards and around, forming a large grey cloud where a small splotch used to be. I became more frantic, scrubbing even harder, until I noticed the ceiling begin to erode. The handprint was gone, but so was most of my paint.

Finally, sweat dripping from my brow, having fallen twice from my chair onto the bed, I stopped and conceded defeat. And, from that day forth, every time I lie in bed, I am reminded of the importance of knowing when to stop cleaning.

If I had been sensible, I could have fallen asleep under the benevolent handprint of my daughter. Instead, I lie awake, staring in regret at the dark, menacing shadow of a cloud.

A bathroom horror story

Editor's note: The following chapter contains material that might be disturbing to some readers. We at HarperCollins were certainly disturbed by it. Reader discretion is advised.

The incident I am about to describe is a little intense, but bear with me, because it contains a powerful moral lesson. And even if it didn't contain a powerful moral lesson, it is cathartic for me to share it with you. If I had to live through such a traumatic experience, the least you can do is read about it.

It happened one chilly Saturday morning just a few months ago. I strolled into my bathroom and noticed that my cat – the carpet frayer – had made a significant deposit in her litter box. I am environmentally conscious, and also extremely lazy, so I use degradable kitty litter that can be flushed down the toilet. I scooped the whole horrible mess into the loo, then threw in a couple of used tissues that were sitting on the vanity. Then I blew my nose into a wad of toilet paper and threw that in the toilet, too. Finally, I pressed the flush, walked out of the bathroom and headed to the kitchen to make a cup of tea.

But before I reached the kettle, I heard a terrible gurgling noise. I ran back to the bathroom and saw, to my horror, that the toilet bowl was filled to the brim with water. And when I say 'water', I mean a horrible mix of water and tissues and toilet paper, and an improbable amount of cat poo. It was certainly more cat poo than I remembered flushing. Had the cat poo somehow multiplied in the toilet? Or had I not paid attention to just how much cat poo I had tried to flush?

The toilet was well and truly blocked. Now, at this point, I should have stopped. I should have come up with a plan. I should have grabbed some matches and lit a fire in the bathroom and burned my entire home to the ground.

But alas, I did the impulsive thing. I looked at the mess in the toilet bowl, thought, *Oh, I'm sure it will go down easily this time*, and pressed the flush again.

Friends, it did not go down. It went up.

When I pressed the flush, the entire toilet exploded. Wave after wave of water infused with kitty litter and cat poo and disgusting wet bits of snotty toilet paper cascaded over my floor. Lamentably, as I was standing directly in front of the toilet, the mess also cascaded all over me. There was kitty litter and cat poo and wet bits of toilet paper on my shoes, on my jeans and on the entirety of the bathroom floor.

Horrifyingly, the bowl was still full. The blockage hadn't shifted at all.

I have a very weak stomach and a sensitive gag reflex. I stood in the middle of this appalling scene gagging and retching uncontrollably. My daughter heard me making 'Gaaaaaggghhh' noises, ran to see what was happening, fell on the floor in the hallway laughing and ran away again. It took me ten minutes to get my retching under control, another ten minutes to unblock the toilet, then fifty-seven minutes (yes, I counted) to clean up the mess in the bathroom. I used every single one of my twelve reusable mop heads. I used two large towels. I used my discarded jeans. I used half a bottle of bleach and another of cleaning spray. I drank two glasses of gin when the whole thing was over, and was still traumatised the next morning.

If you are traumatised, too, I apologise. But I promised you a moral lesson and here it is: life can change in the blink of an eye, and bad things (like exploding toilets) can happen to good people (like me). So many of us are striving for perfection instead of appreciating the good fortune we have now. It is tragic that we fail to recognise the beauty in our lives until something terrible happens (like an exploding toilet).

Stop worrying so much about making your house immaculate, and appreciate the clean-enough home you have now. If your bathroom floor is free of kitty litter and poo, you have everything you could possibly need.

Timeline: Washing the windows

2.35 pm: Arrive home full of energy, which may or may not have something to do with the extra strong cappuccino I drank at lunch. The sun is out, and I notice that the glass sliding doors to my balcony are water-spotted and grubby after a week of rain. I will clean them, I decide. I am motivated! I am ready!

2.40 pm: Get out the window cleaning spray, a cloth and a step stool. I am energised! I am enthusiastic! I will get those windows sparkling clean!

2.42 pm: Start on the balcony side of the first of the four glass panels. Spray on, wipe off! Spray on, wipe off! I'm getting it done! I'm excited!

3.07 pm: Wipe my brow. On the third of the four glass panels. Now not quite as excited. I am running out of steam.

3.13 pm: Have cleaned all four of the glass doors. I am a domestic goddess! I am a superstar! Step back to survey my work. With the brilliant sun behind me, the glass looks fantastic. I've finished! Job well done. I am exhausted. Time for another coffee.

3.14 pm: Realise I have only cleaned one side of the glass.

3.15 pm: Move on to the living-room side of the glass. With the sunlight streaming in, I can see that the doors are still grimy. I guess the coffee will have to wait.

3.34 pm: I am spraying. I am wiping. Spray on. Wipe bloody off. No matter how much I polish, the glass is still smeary. Why is it smeary? Why isn't it getting clean? What am I doing wrong?

3.46 pm: Running back and forth in a deranged frenzy between the balcony and living-room side of the sliding doors. I cannot remove the smears from the glass. I can see the streaks from where I've sprayed and wiped. Why won't it get clean? WHY WON'T IT GET CLEAN?

4.02 pm: Have been cleaning for hours. I am dripping with sweat. My arms are sore. I curse my glass doors!

Who even needs to see outside? My back yard isn't all that exciting.

4.17 pm: I'm done. I can't take anymore. My arms are killing me. I walk back into the living room. The glass looks OK. It will have to do.

4.24 pm: Hear the crack of thunder. Look out the glass doors. The skies are black. It starts to pour.

EIGHT

Mess loves company: how to delegate

A note for women

Though this book is inclusive, and I welcome readers of all genders, this chapter is specifically for women. It discusses cleaning in relation to hormonal fluctuations and the challenges of aging. If you do not identify as a woman or this topic doesn't interest you, please just go ahead and skip to page 178: 'Make cleaning more fun'. Thank you so much for reading, and I'll see you soon! Women, turn the page.

OK. Have the men gone? Brilliant. Now listen up, ladies. We are going to be smashing the patriarchy.

I don't mean to get all political with you, but cleaning is a feminist issue. We cannot discuss housework, or how to delegate chores, without acknowledging the unfair burden on women. Women do far more cleaning than their male partners, even when both are in full-time employment. This gender gap in housework is a remnant of a bygone era, in which men went out to work and women stayed home, raised children and perfected their lemon tart.

Now, cleaning itself isn't an anti-feminist act. Cleaning is just the act of picking up a sponge (or a mop, or a broom) and removing some grime and dirt. Still, the cultural pressure to keep a beautiful home is a tool of patriarchal oppression, because it is women, not men, who shoulder most of the burden of cleaning and tidying the house. All those influencers with their aspirational pantries and their perfectly decluttered homes and their whiter-than-white whites are to the home-management space what the Kardashians are to beauty. The standards they perpetuate are just as unrealistic, and it is mainly us women who internalise them. The unending pressure to live up to these standards makes us feel inadequate and ashamed of our homes, and the time spent on housework keeps us from focusing on finding fulfilment in other areas of our lives.

I could quote you statistics, but statistics are boring, so instead I will ask you some questions.

How many men do you know who won't rest when they're tired because they need to finish cleaning the house?

How many men do you know who google 'How to clean a shower screen' or 'How to remove avocado stains from clothes?'

How many men do you know who madly tidy up for guests and say, 'Please excuse the mess!' when they arrive?

Maybe one? Maybe two? It is certainly a minority. It is overwhelmingly women who follow the home-organisation influencers. It is overwhelmingly women who read the cleaning blogs. And it is overwhelmingly women who notice mess around the home and rush in with their brooms and their pans.

'Oh, but my husband just doesn't notice mess!' my girlfriends say, and they really do seem to believe it. Their husbands have defective eyes, or their husbands have defective brains, or perhaps their husbands are just genetically programmed not to notice dishes in the kitchen sink.

But these same men, who are mysteriously blind to wet towels on the floor, will notice the tiniest scratches on their cars or motorbikes, with magnified, laser-sharp focus. There is clearly nothing wrong with their eyes or their brains; it is all just cultural conditioning. They have internalised the blokey value of a pristine car, and simply couldn't care less about a clean bathroom.

If you genuinely can't rest until your house is spotless, it is worth asking yourself why. If your self-esteem is tied up in the cleanliness of your home, try to challenge your beliefs about women and housework. If you feel like a bad person because your house is messy, at least ask yourself if that is true.

You can't force the men in your life to take on more of the housework (although my delegating tips will help you try). You can, however, refuse to do it all yourself and begin to tolerate mess. The less cleaning you do, the more you change the status quo, and the more you chip away at the patriarchy.

And ladies, taking down the patriarchy is really hard work. Make sure you follow it up with a cup of tea and a nice lie down. You need to keep up your strength.

Make cleaning more fun

Men, welcome back! After that little discussion of hormones, we are now going to be diving into the delegation of chores.

If you live with other people, they should be pulling their weight around the house. It is not fair for one person to do all the cleaning, nor is it fair for the people who live with you to treat you like a maid. (The exception, of course, is if you *are* a live-in maid, in which case it is perfectly appropriate to be treated as such. But if you are a live-in maid, perhaps don't reveal to your employers that you are reading a book about the life-changing magic of mess.)

You will increase the likelihood of other members of your household sharing in the chores if you can make those chores sound palatable, and even fun. Instead of suggesting, for example, that someone 'clean the toilet', ask instead that they 'polish the throne'. Cleaning the toilet sounds menial, and is associated with bodily waste, whereas polishing the throne sounds terribly elegant and evokes a sense of great luxury and wealth.

No one in your family will wish to 'mop the floor', a wet and grotty task. If you propose, instead, that they 'wash down the crime scene', you'll create a thrilling sense of urgency, and hint menacingly at a jail sentence if the chore is not completed. Similarly, no one will be enthused when asked to 'take out the trash'. But if you request that they 'quickly remove the evidence', they will be immediately intrigued and will make haste before the dog squad appears.

'Go change the sheets' sounds dreadfully tedious and involves a difficult tussle with a fitted sheet. But 'dress the bedchamber' is wonderfully sexy and has eighteenth-century castle vibes. 'Unpacking the groceries' is boring, thankless, and takes about seventy-five hours. But 'stowing the bounty' is delightfully triumphant, and suggests a treasure trove of wonders inside the recyclable shopping bags.

Finally, no one in your home is interested in 'doing the laundry'. It is hard work and time-consuming and, frankly, it's drudgery. But 'preparing the finery' is deeply romantic, with hints of bodices and an evening ball. Just throw out the suggestion and watch as your family race each other to the washing machine.

Reframe the narrative. Lure in your helpers. A little bit of manipulation can go a surprisingly long way.

Chore compliance strategies

In an ideal world, all the members of your household would look around the house, notice what needed cleaning, and do it without being asked. (Actually, in an ideal world, you'd have a self-cleaning house, but 'do it without being asked' is the next best thing.)

Sadly, in this actual world, you probably need to ask – and even plead – for other people in your house to pull their weight. Well, I am here to help. As a mother of three kids (and as the ex-wife of their father), I have considerable expertise in this area of household management. I have extensive experience in asking for help around the house, and even greater familiarity with having my requests for help ignored. I have tried every possible strategy to get my family to do their chores, and have even had one or two successes over the years.

Some strategies are effective, some strategies are entirely ineffective, and one strategy is borderline illegal, but I have outlined them all helpfully for you below.

Strategy 1: Using a roster

When drawing up a roster, the head of the household assigns tasks to each person, notes these tasks on a handy spreadsheet or calendar, then sticks the roster on the fridge. Some creative household managers choose to colour-code their rosters, or use interesting fonts, or add stickers or gold stars. None of these adornments has any impact on compliance, but the gold stars distract nicely from the mess.

Advantages: A roster is relatively simple to make and can be a fun artistic outlet for people who enjoy writing on posters with coloured pens. Furthermore, a roster on the fridge demonstrates your authority and adds a note of gravitas to both your fridge and your home.

Disadvantages: The authority and gravitas is a complete illusion, and no one will read your roster. The rest of your household will walk right past it on their way to leave dishes in the sink.

Overall effectiveness: 2/5

Strategy 2: Nagging

Nagging is the repeated pestering of people to do what you want them to do. In previous generations, nagging was limited to phone calls or face-to-face conversations. With the advent of smartphones, nagging can now extend to texts, private messages, emails, voice messages and shaming posts on social media.

Advantages: Nagging is free and requires no special equipment other than your voice and a mobile phone. You can nag at your own convenience, or schedule nagging for critical junctures during the day (for example, after dinner when the dishes need washing).

Disadvantages: Other household members may become desensitised to your voice and may ignore you or delete your messages. You may start to hate the sound of your own nagging and begin to deeply resent your own texts. You will certainly start to resent the people you find yourself nagging.

Oh, and it doesn't work.

Overall effectiveness: 1/5

Strategy 3: Pleading

Pleading is what happens when nagging doesn't work, and you are at the end of your ability to cope. When you plead, you don't ask people what to do; you beg them, dramatically, with hand gestures and tears.

Advantages: If you can generate genuine emotion then pleading can be extremely effective. Very few people can hold out against a loved one who is broken and crying on the floor. Your family, partner or housemates will rush to help you amid sincere apologies and promises to do better in the future.

Disadvantages: Pleading will work only once in a blue moon, as people quickly become desensitised to weeping. What's more, pleading is psychologically draining for the pleader, especially if you cry real tears. Save this one for emergency use only.

Overall effectiveness: 3/5

Strategy 4: Bribery

Bribery involves offering a cash or gift incentive to get someone to do what you want them to do. It is a controversial technique when used on children, and even more controversial when used on adults. It is essential that you understand the person's currency: what it is that they want that you can leverage to your advantage.

Advantages: Bribery works. If you can figure out the person's currency (Gifts? Cash? More screen time? Sex?) and you are willing and able to provide it, you'll have them doing whatever you desire.

Disadvantages: Bribery encourages people to help around the house for personal gain instead of for the intrinsic joy of being a contributing member of the household.

Advantages: Did I mention it works?

Disadvantages: If you are paying cash or offering other commercial incentives, bribery will cost you money.

Advantages: Yeah, yeah. It works.

Disadvantages: Friends and family might look down on you for bribing your kids or partner.

Advantages: WHO CARES, IT WORKS.

Overall effectiveness: 4.5/5

Strategy 5: Punishment

Punishment is like bribery in reverse: instead of handing out a reward to someone who does their chores, you impose a consequence on someone who does not. Again, you need to know the person's currency, and you must be prepared to follow through.

Advantages: Punishments are free, easy to access and don't require any special skills.

Disadvantages: Punishments can be extremely inconvenient for the person doling them out. Sure, you sound powerful and authoritative when you threaten to turn off the Wi-Fi if your child fails to clean up her room. But the joke is on you when she doesn't clean up her room, and you have to turn off the Wi-Fi, and your kid is angry and bored, and she is demanding attention and telling you you're a mean mother, and you just want to nap on the couch.

And punishment can escalate awfully quickly when you use it on an adult. You start by confiscating your partner's golf clubs when he leaves his clothes on the floor, he retaliates by hiding your car keys, you retaliate by throwing his clothes out the window, and the next thing you know you're consulting a divorce lawyer – and trust me, divorce lawyers are expensive. You're far better off nipping the whole thing in the bud and hiring a cleaner instead.

Overall effectiveness: 1/5

Strategy 6: Force
Using physical force can be tempting, especially when you live with a mad toddler, or a know-it-all teen, or a partner of any age at all.

Advantages: It's certainly impactful.

Disadvantages: No! Don't do it! Violence is never the answer. (At least, it's not the answer to mess.)

Overall effectiveness: 0/5

Strategy 7: Going on strike

Instead of nagging, or pleading, or bribing, or punishing, or using violence (which you won't, because violence is never the answer!), you always have the option of going on strike. Don't get angry. Don't make threats. Simply stop doing the housework. If the other members of your household want clean clothes, or clean crockery, or fresh linen, or a pleasant toilet, they will have to sort it out themselves.

Advantages: As you will no longer be burdened with housework or laundry, you will be free to spend your spare time watching movies and drinking wine on the couch. What's more, it is possible that your strike will motivate those around you to get off their own couches and pull their weight.

Disadvantages: It is also possible that no one in your household will crave clean clothes, clean crockery, fresh linen, or a pleasant toilet strongly enough to do something about it. It is eminently possible that after a week of you being on strike, you will all be wallowing in your own filth.

Advantages: At least you will be wallowing in filth while watching movies and drinking wine on the couch.

Overall effectiveness: 4.5/5

NINE

A broom in the hand is worth two in the bush: equipment

Things you don't need

Once you have determined what needs to be cleaned, and you have ~~manipulated~~ motivated your family to do their fair share, it is time to stock up on the right equipment.

If you read the cleaning books and home-management blogs and Instagram posts, you'll be forgiven for believing you need a small army of appliances to successfully maintain your home. This is, of course, just Big Cleaning propaganda. People cleaned their homes for thousands of years without Super Max Turbo sweepers and cordless bionic mops and specialist cleaning 'systems'. When I was growing up, my mother washed the dishes with rags torn from her petticoat, she swept the floors with a broom made from her own hair, and she used a cleaning solution that was one-third vinegar, one-third lemon juice and one-third the bitter tears of her children.

These days, however, there is a steady stream of new appliances to help you clean your home in highly advanced and extremely complex ways. Perhaps the most famous example is the robot vacuum cleaner, that dust-sucking disc on wheels. The robot vacuum cleaner is to the cleaning world what the Thermomix is to cooking: expensive, complicated, fantastically hyped, and loved and loathed in equal measure.

How do you know if a person has a robot vacuum cleaner? They will a) tell you, and b) introduce you to the robot when you come to visit.

'Meet Sir Cleanalot,' they will gush, smiling affectionately at the machine, or, 'Check out Robo Cop over here!'

When the robot gets stuck in a shagpile rug – which it inevitably will – they will exclaim, 'Oops! Seems the Dust Meister has got himself in a pickle!' or, 'Come on, Fred, let's get you moving again.'

And when the robot grinds to a halt in the middle of the house, they will rush to its aid as though a beloved child has fallen ill.

'Oh Roberto!' they will coo. 'What on Earth has happened? Let's get you back into your base.'

A robot vacuum cleaner might make an endearing pet, but it is expensive and wholly unnecessary. So too is the Crosswave Cordless and the Spotclean Turbo and the ProHeat Revolution Two. Friends do not let friends buy portable upholstery-cleaning machines, or UV sanitising lights, or rechargeable scrubbers with seven different attachment heads. You do not need a specialised sliding-door-track cleaning brush to clean your sliding-door track, and you certainly do not need a sterilising box for your mobile phone when you can wipe it down with some petticoat and tears.

All these fancy appliances can lead you down a dangerous, slippery slope to pointless high-tech hell. You'll start with a Wi-Fi-enabled, three-in-one robot window cleaner, move on to a flying hoverboard and a hands-free umbrella drone, and then suddenly you're investing in dodgy cryptocurrency and investigating post-mortem cryogenic freezing. It is far safer to stick with a standard vacuum cleaner and a classic broom and pan.

It's hard to determine whether a whiz-bang contraption is the miracle product it is hyped to be. So, to help you figure out if a new device is worth buying, please refer to the list below.

Editor's note: Our fact-checker informs us that there is no record of the author's mother having created a broom from her own hair. According to neighbours, she owned a very nice Hoover Dial-a-Matic vacuum.

You definitely, positively, one hundred per cent do not need:

- The latest cult purchase!
- The viral machine that has wowed fans on TikTok!
- The new appliance that's breaking the internet!
- The multi-purpose machine that everyone is talking about!
- The six-in-one system that will change the way you clean!
- The cleaning tool that busy mums can't get enough of!
- The time-saving gadget that people are going wild for!
- The bestselling gizmo that lives up to its hype!

Things you do need

As an aspirational home-management influencer, I am often asked about my skincare routine. (Actually, this isn't true. No one has ever asked me about this.) I am also regularly asked about my home-management routine. (Actually, this isn't true either. No one even knows I am a home-management influencer. Frankly, I didn't even know until a month ago.)

Still, although you have not asked, I have answered. Please find below my top ten essentials for keeping my house acceptably clean. You will note that I do not use expensive high-tech cleaning equipment, and I do not use cleaning solutions other than vinegar and bicarb. (Ha ha. I'm only joking about the vinegar and bicarb – I have tried it and it doesn't work nearly as well as the toxic cleaning sprays that give off poisonous fumes.)

Top ten home management essentials

1. A cleaner

Hiring a cleaner is the absolute best investment that you can make in your mental health and relationships. If it is at all possible; if there is any way you can afford it; if there is anything you can give up so that you can afford it; if there is anything or anyone that you can sell so that you can afford it – invest in a cleaner. Even a couple of hours a fortnight from a professional cleaner will significantly take the edge off your housework burden. And, as an added benefit, when you have guests in your home you can gesture to your mess and say nonchalantly, 'Oh, the cleaner will deal with this tomorrow', and your visitors will nod sagely and move on. (Of course, this line works equally whether you actually have a cleaner or not.)

I recognise that not everyone can afford a cleaner. If you cannot, I encourage you to return this book to the store and use the cash refund to hire a cleaner for an hour.

If you are lucky enough to afford a cleaner, please don't fall into the 'must clean up for the cleaner' nonsense. You do not need to clean up for a cleaner any more than you need to bake bread to take to the bakery, or assign your maths teacher some algebra homework, or offer a waiter at the café a glass of wine. It is the cleaner's job to clean your home, and *your* job is to facilitate that process by getting out of their way.

Editor's note: Please do not return this book to the store. You cannot return a book that you have read. Also, we at HarperCollins believe that a book is infinitely more valuable than an hour of sweeping and scouring.

2. Lots of doors

Doors are truly the unsung heroes of the home-management space. Simply open a door, throw your mess behind it, and voilà, the mess is gone! Closing a door is truly the ultimate low-tech cleaning hack of our time.

Doors are ostensibly for privacy, but this doesn't bear scrutiny. Do your cans of tuna need privacy in the pantry? Does your organic deodorant need privacy in the bathroom cabinet? Do your gumboots need privacy on the floor of your wardrobe? No, of course not! Doors exist to hide mess.

Your house cannot have too many doors. If you have a spare wall or a corner, build a cupboard with a door. If you have a room and a doorway, it needs a door. Hell, if you have a large enough room, put a door in the middle! The more doors you have, the more areas of your home can be shut off to enclose your mess.

Once you close your doors, try to open them only when essential. Your goal is to completely banish the mess from your mind, to forget that it even exists. And trust me, this is surprisingly easy! I still get a surprise when I open our living-room cupboard to find the range of clutter that is inside.

Doors are particularly useful when you are entertaining visitors and wish to convey an impression of order. Just usher your guests straight into your living area and keep the rest of your home firmly hidden away. Don't even think about giving guests a tour of your home; you are not a small-town mayor trying to drum up tourism business. Just offer them a glass of wine and plenty of chocolate biscuits and they will lose their curiosity entirely.

Now, I have noticed that some parents will threaten to remove the door to their teenager's bedroom as a punishment for bad behaviour. I am, as you know, extremely non-judgemental when it comes to parenting choices. There is no right or wrong when it comes to raising a child; whatever works for you and your family is the right way to go. But removing a teenager's door? My God! Teen bedrooms are dens of horror and depravity and should be firmly shut off from the rest of the house. Your eyes should not be burdened by the atrocities within. Your emotional wellbeing comes before your teen's disciplinary needs. Save yourselves, my friends! Save yourselves and shut the door.

3. *Several throw rugs*

A throw rug is a good option for those areas in your home where you cannot easily install a door – your living-room couch, for example, or your child's bedroom floor, or your bed. You just gather all your mess into one big pile, throw a rug over it, and presto! The room immediately looks clean.

4. *Baby wipes*

Baby wipes are gentle, pre-moistened towelettes designed to clean a baby's tiny little bum. At least, that's what the product description says on the packet. In fact, baby wipes are a miracle invention that can dust, scour and remove stubborn stains. I have no idea what powerful ingredients are in baby wipes – and, frankly, I don't want to find out – but those innocuous-looking wipes in the pop-up pack can get almost any surface spotlessly clean.

Of course, baby wipes aren't great for the environment, and they're probably quite toxic for your baby. I've seen a baby wipe dissolve an oil patch on a carpet; presumably, it could also dissolve part of your child. Still, they are the ultimate cleaning accessory and, best of all, you don't even need a baby to buy them!

Baby wipes are one of the great open secrets of the home-management space, rarely acknowledged by influencers for fear their entire industry will be made defunct. How do you get finger marks off a wall? Baby wipes! Best way to dust your knick-knacks? Baby wipes! How to get stains off a carpet? Baby wipes! How to vacuum your floors? Well, obviously baby wipes can't do that, but you get the idea. How to clean your house? Baby wipes! (Just don't ever use them on an actual baby. Those wipes are strong.)

5. Baby powder
Baby powder lifts oil stains out of anything, and it smells delightfully fresh. (Side note: what is it with the cleaning power of products meant for babies?)

6. A coffee machine
Obviously, a coffee machine will not clean your house. A coffee machine will, however, make coffee, and coffee cleanses your soul and washes away your pain. You need the healing and elevating powers of caffeine in order to

effectively perform your household chores. Take all the money you would have spent on a Turbo 500 Triple Suction Vacuum Supermop and spend it on a De'Longoria Super-Charged Bean Boiler or a Crema Quattrocinque Extra Espresso 1000. And buy some nice coffee cups while you're at it. You'll want to savour every drop.

7. Decent headphones

If you must do housework, you need to be able to listen to some music, or at least an educational podcast on celebrity gossip. Time passes much more quickly when you are singing along to the latest catchy tune about oral sex, or learning which two celebs are consciously uncoupling, which celeb is reuniting with an ex, which celeb is back in rehab, and which celeb's racist/sexist/homophobic tweet from seven years ago has re-emerged.

8. An iron

Haha, no. You don't need an iron! Don't be ridiculous! I was just checking to see if you were paying attention. Buy things that don't crease or don't buy them at all. Who the hell has time for ironing?

9. Messy friends

Now, this one is important, and I'll explain why. Have you ever been out to dinner with a bunch of friends, and when the waiter asks if anyone wants dessert you all look questioningly at each other? You are dying to order the Exploding Chocolate Mousse Cake with Vanilla Bean Ice Cream, but then Mandy shakes her head, and then Carole says no, and then Lisa says, 'Not for me', and of course you can't eat dessert alone! And so you sadly put down the menu, with the dream of chocolate mousse fading, and regretfully tell the waiter, 'No, just the bill, thanks.'

But if Janine had got in first and said, 'Ooh, yes, I'll have the apple pie', then Lisa would have ordered the cheesecake, and Carole would have ordered the pavlova, and you could have had your chocolate mousse, and Mandy would have asked for an extra spoon.

My point is this: attitudes are contagious. If all your friends are neat, you are going to feel pressured into being neat, too. If most of your friends are shambolic, you are going to feel much more comfortable with your mess.

Of course, you can still be friends with neat people. There are neat people in the world who have many fine qualities, provided you wipe your feet thoroughly before entering their home and always put your drink down on a coaster. But be sure to cultivate deep and enduring friendships with messy people, too. (Also, you must be sure to maintain friendships with people who always order dessert, but I think that goes without saying.)

10.   *Alcohol and chocolate*
This really needs no further explanation.

TEN

Laugh and the world laughs with you, clean and you clean alone: how to manage your household

The opposite of a schedule

Home-management influencers thrive on schedules. Go to any cleaning blog (or don't; I certainly try not to) and you'll find a free, downloadable, colour-coded housework schedule in handy PDF form. These schedules are detailed, prescriptive and excruciatingly dull, and I haven't yet read one through to the end. From what I can gather, specific chores are allocated to each day of the week. Once a week you do the more time-consuming jobs, once a month you do a big spring clean, and on a rest day you just do the laundry.

Now, aside from the egregiousness of a rest day including laundry (I mean, if laundry was restful, it would be called 'a nap'), I am not in favour of cleaning schedules. For one thing, a schedule is unsustainable, like that exercise bike you purchased on impulse during a pandemic. You greet it with excitement, you use it once or twice, and then it lays dormant in your room for a year.

For another thing, a cleaning schedule can damage your self-esteem. Sure, it's wonderfully affirming when you complete your day's chores and cross everything smugly off your list. But when you don't get through your tasks, that rigid, pompous schedule will chastise you from across the room.

And finally, we human beings just aren't designed for strict schedules. We are creatures of the universe! We are children of nature! We vibrate with energy and with hormonal fluctuations! We cannot be forced into an artificial schedule that takes no heed of our emotional needs.

Instead of imposing a housework schedule on yourself, try experimenting with 'intuitive cleaning'. Intuitive cleaning is the opposite of a restrictive cleaning schedule. It doesn't tell you what to clean on any given day or week. Intuitive cleaning asks that you tune into yourself and follow your own natural rhythms and desires. Only you can decide when it's time to change the sheets, or do the laundry, or scrub the bathroom floor. Intuitive cleaning makes *you* the expert on housework, and encourages you to clean according to your mood.

Now, I cannot tell you how to perform intuitive cleaning. You need to venture forth on your personal cleaning journey alone. I can, however, offer a suggested framework to get you started. Just be mindful of your own needs, moods and cleaning desires, and always let your intuition guide your sponge.

Intuitive cleaning

What to clean when ...

You're angry: Anger gives us a surge of energy and a laser-sharp focus. In evolutionary terms, this energy and focus is designed to help us to hunt down and slay the object of our rage. As the modern world frowns upon most acts of murder, channel your angry energy instead into fiddly household tasks that require concentration and drive. Use your anger to dust, clean the blinds and cornices, and get into those tiny nooks and crannies around your home. Anger is also ideal for scrubbing and scouring, as the repetitive movements are vaguely reminiscent of punching.

You're annoyed with someone in your home: Being annoyed creates the perfect opportunity to wash dishes, empty the dishwasher or even clear the table. Plates and bowls can be slammed satisfyingly on the counter, glasses can be clinked and cutlery clattered. Remember, though, that the aim of slamming plates is to alert the person who you're annoyed with to their wrongdoing. If they take the bait and ask you what's wrong, don't slam another plate and say, 'NOTHING!' Use your words. Own your feelings. Tell them exactly what they've done. And then make them do the bloody dishes.

You're stressed: Stress makes us antsy and is the ideal fuel for soothing, repetitive tasks that don't require a great deal of attention. Use your stress to vacuum, mop, clean windows, wipe down surfaces and dust. Remember, though, that stress can make you easily distracted and careless, so avoid delicate areas of your home that can be damaged by overcleaning. (Bedroom ceilings, for example. Who knew that paint could so easily erode?)

You're feeling overwhelmed: Overwhelm creates a perfect opportunity to do laundry. It is easy, takes up little brain space and gives you an immediate sense of achievement.

You're feeling sad: When you're feeling sad, change your sheets. It is always extremely comforting to have crisp, clean sheets. Also, after you've finished changing the sheets, you can throw yourself on the bed and have a therapeutic cry.

You're excited or nervous: Excitement gives us a rush of adrenalin and makes it hard to sit still, or even stand in one spot, let alone focus on completing one task. This is the ideal state in which to tidy up the mess strewn all over your home. Just run around the house in whatever direction your nerves take you, picking up items and putting them back where they belong.

You're bored: Are you restless? Listless? Unsure how to fill the hours? Do you feel uncomfortable sitting with yourself in quiet contemplation? Take the opportunity to get to work sorting and filing all those papers that have been piling up on your hall table for months. After ten to twenty minutes, you will pine for those sweet moments of boredom, and learn to cherish sitting in solitude with nothing to do.

You are happy and content: This is the only safe time to tackle cleaning the fridge. If you are feeling calm, you can unpack the fridge and wipe it out without stress-eating that three-day-old schnitzel or diving into that questionable block of cheese.

You're scared: Clean the bathroom. There is no particular reason to clean the bathroom when you're scared, but it's always good to have a clean bathroom, and you may as well turn your fear into a positive.

You're on a deadline: This is the perfect time to stop whatever you're doing and start reorganising your pantry.

Top tips for home organisation

Embracing the joy of mess means respecting your own personal organisational systems, even if they seem random and chaotic to an outsider. Just as I encourage you to follow your intuition in cleaning, I encourage you to follow your intuition in organising. There is no 'right' way to organise your pantry or wardrobe, nor is there a 'best' way to store all your stuff. If you want to keep your shoes in the vegetable crisper in your fridge, stick your unpaid bills on the mirror in your bathroom, or hang your books next to your dry goods in your bedroom closet, then all power to you for your innovation.

I am asked about my organisational systems and practices about as frequently as I am asked about my skincare regime (which, as you know, is never). Still, I am an aspirational home-management influencer after all, and so I feel compelled to share with you my own home-organisation tips and tricks. Read them and appreciate them, but please don't follow them. I do not wish to stifle your own innate creativity.

1. Organising my fridge

I have an extremely efficient system for organising my fridge. When I buy perishable food, I put it in the fridge. When I want to eat something that is in the fridge, I take it out of the fridge. When I spy a mildewing pile of vegetables, or leftovers from last month, or dairy products that smell funny, or sliced meats that have gone furry, I take them out of the fridge and throw them in the bin. (Once, just once, I tried a bite of the leftovers, but I'll never be doing that again.)

2. Organising my pantry

Now, I thought very carefully about how to arrange my pantry – there were so many options to consider! I could have organised my goods according to the size of the packaging, or perhaps the colour, shape, or even texture. I could have sorted my food according to taste, dividing it into sweet versus savoury, or really delicious versus healthy. Instead, I decided to settle on a compromise and chose a combination of all the above. I put the square things to the left, the red boxes in the middle, the big packets on the right, the sweet things in the front, and the healthy items right at the back. This creates a sense of variety and interest and keeps all my family members on their toes.

3. Organising my linen closet

My sheets don't know if they've been balled up or folded, and neither do any of us who sleep on them. I simply shove them firmly in the linen press and pull them out again as needed.

4. Organising the kids' toy cupboard

When my kids were young, I did not organise their toy cupboard. Why would I have organised their toy cupboard? Never in their lives did any of my kids open the toy cupboard. Even when they were old enough to understand the concept of object permanence, they only played with the toys that were already out on the floor. My daughter might have played passionately with her Barbie, for example, but if I put it in the toy cupboard, she forgot all about it, and played with her drum kit instead. (The exception, of course, is when I threw out her Barbie, at which point she immediately asked for it, declaring it her favourite toy in the world.)

5. Organising my wardrobe

As you already know, I hang everything in my wardrobe. What you may not know is that this includes that most supportive of garments: my bras.

Apparently hanging one's bras is not a common practice, which shows that most home–management

influencers aren't quite as innovative as they believe. I learned this after a rather humiliating working-from-home fail during the recent catastrophic global pandemic. I was doing a live television interview from my bedroom in the middle of a lockdown, and when I caught a glimpse of myself on the Zoom window my heart fell out of my chest. And 'chest' was the operative word because, in the background, my wardrobe was open, revealing my bras hanging on their 3M hooks inside the door.

Now, clearly I had broken my own rule about keeping doors closed. Do as I say, not as I do! But after the incident, something extraordinary happened. Women all over the country wrote to me to tell me I had changed their lives; that from now on they, too, would be hanging their bras on hooks. They believed me to be some kind of wardrobe pioneer. A Barbara! A BarBra, if you will!

Of course, you know I just hang my bras because I am lazy and do not like drawers. But my bra-hanging (branging?) revolution proved two things. Firstly, mess is the way of the future. Messy people, this is our time in the sun!

And secondly, you really should check your background during Zoom calls. Preferably before you are on air.

6.   Organising my bookshelf

My take on organising books is a little controversial. I don't classify books as fiction versus non-fiction, or sci-fi versus romance novel, or crime thriller versus comedy. To me, books fall into one of only two categories: books I love, and books I don't. I put the books I love on my bookshelf in whatever order I have read them. The books I don't love pile up by the front door. If you'd like one, please let me know.

7.   Organising my bedside drawer

Just kidding! Of course I don't organise my bedside drawer! That would be super weird. I just throw everything inside, take things out once in a while, and pray that no one ever looks in there but me.

Timeline: Doing a spring clean

10.00 am: It is a rainy Saturday morning and my kids are all out. The house is a mess. It is a perfect day for a spring clean!

10.18 am: Download a cleaning schedule from a website called *My House Is Cleaner Than Your House.* It is very inspiring.

10.26 am: Peruse the schedule over a cup of coffee. The schedule tells me that I should start by cleaning the kitchen, work my way through the bedrooms, move on to the living area, then finish with the bathrooms and windows. That sounds hard.

10.30 am: Delete the cleaning schedule.

10.32 am: Open YouTube, search 'Cleaning Inspiration', and begin playing an eight-hour video entitled *Cheryl Gets Clean*. An attractive blonde woman appears on screen and I wonder briefly if I have stumbled upon some niche porn.

10.33 am: Nope. It's not porn. Cheryl is actually cleaning her house.

10.35 am: Cheryl is vacuuming her floors. This is not at all inspiring. Turn the video off.

10.36 am: Decide to quickly check Instagram before I start my spring clean.

10.52 am: Wipe away a few tears. Wow. Those reunion videos always make me so emotional.

10.53 am: OK. I am going to start cleaning.

10.54 am: Get out a sponge. I will start with the fridge. I open the fridge. Ooh, cake!

10.58 am: Mmm. This cake is absolutely delicious.

11.02 am: I am definitely going to start cleaning now! I'll just quickly check Twitter.

11.16 am: OK. I am absolutely, truly going to start cleaning now.

11.17 am: Grab a dust cloth and some cleaning spray.

11.18 am: Look around my house. There are papers heaped on the kitchen table and a pile of laundry in the hall. The windows could probably use a sponge and the shelves could do with a dust. The pantry is in a state of disarray. A plastic giraffe lies on the floor.

11.20 am: Look out the window. The rain is clearing. I could be sitting in a coffee shop reading the paper. I could phone my mum and arrange to meet her for lunch. I could go for a walk and listen to a podcast. I could go out to the markets. I could visit a friend.

11.21 am: *Do I really need to clean?* I wonder. The house looks OK.

11.22 am: Put down my dust cloth. No, I think. Not today.

Cleaning hacks

Google 'cleaning hacks' and you will come up with approximately eighty-nine million results. (I know, that's a lot. You're probably going to need a bigger house.)

Cleaning hacks are the flirty younger cousin of the cult purchase. They are playful and fun, they're great to introduce to your friends, and they don't want your money or a lifetime commitment. Cleaning hacks are also a little weird and socially unacceptable, and often involve doing extremely odd things with toothpaste, Coke, old socks, tea, lemon, vodka, hairspray, shaving cream and, of course, vinegar and bicarb.

Most cleaning hacks won't save you much time, though they will possibly save you some money. This depends, however, on the quality of toothpaste you buy, and whether you wear designer-label socks. Cleaning hacks are also entertaining if you're interested in off-brand uses for coffee filters, or enjoy doing fascinating things with dishwasher tablets when you're nowhere near a dishwasher.

Still, even the most viral cleaning hack doesn't change the fundamentals of cleaning. You can't wave a lime and a can of shaving cream at a bathroom and watch it magically transform. Cleaning is laborious and unpleasant even when you're using hacks; if it wasn't, I'd be doing much more of it.

Still, there are a handful of cleaning hacks that will dramatically reduce the amount of cleaning required in your home. Now, these hacks are not listed on any cleaning influencer's website, nor will you find them in any other book. There is no profit to be gained from any of these hacks; they cannot be monetised or sold. Up until now, they have remained a closely guarded secret that could bring down the whole cleaning industry. I share them here with you against the entreaties of Big Cleaning; I just hope that they reach you in time.

Three cleaning hacks that actually work

1. Find a partner who loves to clean

This is a truly life-changing hack; perhaps the greatest investment you can make in your journey to avoid cleaning. However, exercise caution: you don't want a partner who is obsessively neat, as that could get intensely annoying. What you want is a partner who gains satisfaction from cleaning up — specifically, satisfaction from cleaning up after you and any shared pets or kids.

Now, if you have already invested in a partner who *doesn't* love to clean, consider trading them in for a new, improved model. There may be some short-term emotional cost involved, but it will definitely pay off in the future.

2. Don't have children

Kids are born messy, and I mean this literally. Have you ever seen someone give birth? There's just mess all over the place, coming from every single orifice. And let me tell you: your child will not get tidier after that. My daughter was born in a flood of blood and gore and, honestly, it was the neatest day of her life. She is just a grot machine, trailing crumbs and food wrappers and slime and nail polish all over the house.

Save yourself. Stay child-free and avoid the unending cascade of filth that emanates from young children. (If it's too late and you've already had a child or two, please refer to Hack Number 1.)

3. Don't have pets.

I have a cat and she is extremely destructive. Penny rips up the upholstery, she pulls up the rug, she sheds hair all over the furniture, she scatters her kitty litter throughout the apartment and she deposits lizard carcasses under my bed. Worse, she expresses her dissatisfaction with whatever food I dare to offer by gobbling it down, growling like a bear, then vomiting it up in the middle of the carpet. Penny is adorable and we love her, but she is a complete menace to our home, and I can only imagine the havoc that would be wreaked by a dog.

Stay away from pets! They are weapons of home destruction! (If it's too late and you already have a pet or two, you know what you must do.)

Have your mess and eat it, too

One of the great design flaws of the human being is our constant need for food. Preparing food generates more domestic mess than any other household activity (with the possible exception of a home water birth, of which, happily, I have no direct experience).

I can keep the mess in my home down to a manageable level, until I attempt to cook dinner. Even the most basic of meals leaves me with dirty utensils, sticky benchtops, splatters of oil and a spattering of crumbs, and that's just from taking the ingredients out of the pantry. By the time I've finished cooking I'm surrounded by crusty pots, smeared plates, dripping oven trays, a spotted splashback and the lingering smell of beef curry and regret.

My mother always taught me that the best way to deal with cooking mess is to clean up as you go along. What my mum failed to appreciate is that 'cleaning up as you go along' is still cleaning, and I very much dislike cleaning.

What's more, when it comes to cooking, the cost-benefit ratio doesn't really stack up in my favour. I spend an hour or more cooking the meal and washing the dishes, only for my kids to inhale their food in ten minutes. And then the very next day – or, sometimes, later that night – they are hungry and want feeding again! I suspect I'd be far more enthusiastic about cooking if my kids required meals just occasionally, as a treat.

Now, it is a radical move to reject cooking culture these days, perhaps more radical even than embracing mess. We live in the age of celebrity chefs, competitive cake-baking and TV shows where amateur cooks regularly break down and weep. And, of course, there's our obsession with posting photos of food on Instagram, with hashtags like #foodporn and #instafood and #healthyeating and #yum. I am still bemused by the motivation of people who post pictures of their pasta online. I spend more time looking at photos of random dinners than I spend looking at the people who ate them.

Still, I am nothing if not radical, and if my work can help just one person, then being a cooking pariah will have been worth it. And so, I am sharing with you my favourite recipes for people who really hate cleaning up. Enjoy them, and remember, an oven doesn't need to be used for cooking! It can be used simply to warm up your takeout.

Recipes for people who hate cleaning

Mess-free dinner for the entire family

Ingredients

A smartphone

Method

1. Pick up your smartphone.
2. Load your phone with a meal delivery app.
3. Choose a style of cuisine that all members of your household will enjoy. (Note: this step is tricky and if performed indelicately can result in outbursts of 'You know I hate sushi!' or 'I'm so sick of pizza' or 'Why does Michael always get to choose?')
4. Order the meal and watch your app eagerly for updates. (Your meal is on its way!)
5. Listen out for the doorbell.

Open your front door and receive your dinner.

Washing up

None, if you eat out of the containers.

Banana Surprise

Ingredients

One banana

Method

1. Carefully peel the banana.

2. Surprise! There's a snack inside!

Washing up

None.

Quick and easy dinner

Ingredients

A box of cereal

Milk (a big slosh)

Method

1. Pour cereal and milk into a bowl.
2. Eat in front of the TV.

Washing up

One bowl and one spoon.

Chocolate sultana clusters

Ingredients

One snack pack of sultanas

One block of dark chocolate

Method

1. Place one piece of chocolate and several sultanas in your mouth.
2. Chew to combine.

Washing up

None.

Chicken noodle soup

Ingredients

One packet of instant chicken noodle soup mix

One cup of boiling water

Method

1. Pour soup mix and water into cup and mix.

2. Put all thoughts of real soup out of your mind.

3. Spoon into your mouth.

Washing up

One mug and one spoon.

Microwave poached eggs

Ingredients

One egg

Method

1. Break egg into a mug.

2. Place mug in microwave.

3. Microwave for thirty to forty seconds.

4. If you hear an explosion, *stop the microwave.*

5. Remove mug.

6. Eat with spoon.

Washing up

This depends on whether the egg exploded in the microwave. If it did not: one mug and one spoon. If it did: one mug and one microwave.

Pad Thai

Ingredients

One pair of legs

Method

1. Walk down the street to your local Thai restaurant.
2. Order takeaway.
3. Walk home again.

Washing up

None, if you eat straight from the containers.

No-bake veggie wheat-cake stack

Ingredients

Two slices of bread

Butter

Salad ingredients (lettuce, tomato, avocado)

Method

1.   Butter the bread.

2.   Place the salad ingredients between the two slices.

3.   Press down to create a stack.

4.   Eat with your hands.

Washing up

One plate and one knife.

Mug cake

Ingredients

One packet of cake mix

Water

Method

1. Scoop a few spoonfuls of the cake mix into a mug.

2. Add a few spoonfuls of water and mix.

3. Microwave for one minute.

4. Ignore the list of toxic ingredients on the packet.

5. Ignore the weird chemical taste.

6. Ignore the unpleasant rubbery texture.

7. Enjoy!

Washing up

One mug and one spoon.

Killer Negroni

Ingredients

30mL gin

30mL Campari

30mL sweet vermouth

Ice

Method

1. Place ice in a glass.

2. Pour other ingredients over the ice.

3. Drink!

Washing up

Yes! Life is messy! But honestly, after drinking this, you won't care.

ELEVEN

Be the mess you want to see in the world: some notes for the mess-challenged

There is hope!

Up until now, I have spoken about the great joys of mess, and the life-threatening perils of tidying up. Still, it is one thing to read an inspirational book about mess; it is quite another to break free from a lifetime of compulsive cleaning. If you are the kind of person who cannot relax unless your house is spotless, the laundry is put away, the pantry is organised and your books are in the correct order, it can be incredibly hard to let go. So, if you're a neat freak or a cleanaholic, how do you learn to appreciate mess?

Well, firstly, if you are a neat freak or a cleanaholic, please note that we do not use those words anymore. The socially appropriate term is 'mess–challenged', or 'person living with neatness'.

Now, if you are a person living with neatness, I want you to know that there is hope for your future. No matter what your background, no matter how often you clean, you too can break free from the shackles of being tidy.

I may seem like a person who was born to make mess, but there is neatness in my genes. My mother is no Barbara Buckman, but she is an energetic household manager (though a cursory glance at her improbable number of vases might suggest otherwise). She is perpetually in a state of motion; buzzing around her house, tidying this and sorting that, her eyes constantly scanning for things to put away. My mother isn't an obsessive cleaner, but she is a queen of tidying up as she goes along; it is a lifestyle for her, and one she proselytises often. She will empty her grocery bags as soon as they enter the house, hang the towels up nicely as soon as she's dried herself after a shower, and fold the laundry the moment it is out of the drier. And, of course, she can get a three-course meal on the table for dinner without leaving a shred of evidence in the kitchen. I can make more mess just eating the food that she has prepared than she will make cooking the entire thing.

My mother is comfortable with clutter, but she would never leave a cupboard door open or leave a wet towel on the floor. She will not put off until tomorrow what she can do today, and she will not leave her house without making the bed. More precisely, she will not leave her *bedroom* without making her bed – unless my father is still in it, which frustrates her no end. Her bed-making is part of her essential morning routine, like drinking a cup of coffee, brushing her teeth and phoning me to ask me if anything bad happened overnight.

With this kind of upbringing, I would be forgiven for being mess-avoidant myself. It is a credit to my commitment to renouncing the burden of perfection that I have become the messy person that I am today. After a childhood spent assiduously tidying up my room, I grew into an adult who can calmly leave her bed in disarray. I feel a quiet sense of achievement that I can destroy my entire kitchen cooking some bolognaise sauce for the kids. I feel a warm glow of pride when looking at the smudges on the mirror, and I smile at the laundry piled high in the hall. When my mum visits my house and immediately starts closing all my cupboards, I realise just how far I have progressed.

If I can overcome my upbringing and embrace the magic of mess, you can overcome your own cleaning habits and do the same. There are steps that you can take to gradually increase your tolerance of disorder and pare down your home management to a minimum.

A twelve-step program for the mess-challenged

1. You admit that you are powerless over your home – that your cleaning has become unmanageable.

2. You come to realise that the solution to your problems is not decluttering systems, or #homeinspo bloggers, or aspirational pantries, or books on spot cleaning, or turbo mops, or cleaning schedules, or jars with calligraphic labels, or even vinegar and bicarb.

3. You make a decision to embrace the healing powers of mess.

4. You make a searching and fearless inventory of your thirty-seven different cleaning sprays, four types of scouring pastes, microfibre cloths, cordless vacuum cleaner, steam mop, dust pans, blog subscriptions, Facebook forum memberships and your notes on 'how to remove tannin stains from teacups' – and you discard them all.

5. You admit to your family, to yourself and to the guests whose plates you whisked away before they had even finished eating, because you couldn't wait to clean the table, that you are obsessive about cleaning.

6. You are ready to stop being obsessive about cleaning and are free to embrace a certain degree of disorder, clutter, grime, crumbs on the counter and streaks on the shower screen.

7. You ask your higher power to remove your passionate desire to colour-code your bookshelves, decant your foodstuffs into Mason jars, fold your fitted sheets in the influencer-approved manner, cull your wardrobe down to the bare minimum and clean out the oven after every meal.

8. You make a list of the people you have harmed by yelling at them to clean their rooms, insisting that they take off their shoes when they enter your home, throwing away their beloved Barbie under the guise of 'decluttering', and looking horrified when they put their glass on the table without using a coaster – and you become willing to make amends to them.

9. You make amends to these people whenever possible, perhaps by allowing them to stay up late on a school night, by letting them put their feet on the couch, by giving them a nice foot massage or by sending them a fruit basket.

10. You continue to take personal inventory, and when you find yourself dusting the skirting boards late at night, or putting hospital corners on the bed, or washing the walls twice a week, or going through your cupboards deciding which items don't spark joy, then you promptly admit it, stop what you're doing, and go take a nap.

11. You constantly seek to improve your relationship with mess; praying for an end to your #homeinspo aspirations, for a tolerance of the slight film of dust on the windowsills, for an acceptance of your overstuffed cupboards and for the power to leave assorted shoes on the living-room floor.

12. Having been liberated from your oppressive cleaning practices, you try to convey the joy of mess to other people living with neatness, and to embrace disorder in your wardrobe, your kitchen, your linen closet, your pantry and your home in general.

Lose the mess stress

It is lamentable indeed that our culture has evolved to celebrate cleanliness and tidiness instead of grime and disorder. There is a parallel universe somewhere – a better, nicer universe – in which mess is aspirational and neat houses are considered second-rate. In this delightful world, Instagram and Facebook reflect a completely different #homeinspo reality. The bloggers and the influencers post inspirational photos of their grotty windowpanes, the wet towels heaped on their bathroom floors and their pantries piled high with tottering towers of expired tinned goods. They use hashtags like #luxurygrot, #MessSweetMess, #cluttergoals, #interiorchaos and #disorderofinstagram.

Alas, we do not live in this heavenly alternate reality, but in a world in which we are all supposed to be striving for perfection. And when we don't achieve perfection – which we often don't, because it is *exhausting* – then we can feel profoundly stressed and ashamed.

I recognise that it is hard to combat the cultural propaganda that tells you that beauty exists in a sparkling shower screen, and that total fulfilment is but a vacuum cleaner away. Still, if you are a person bravely living with neatness, there is a way out of this prison. To overcome your social conditioning, the messages you tell yourself need to be stronger than the messages you are absorbing from others. You can rewire your brain to accept imperfection, and I have developed a patented Three-Step Mess Desensitisation Program™ specifically to show you how.

Editor's note: Nope, this one isn't patented either.

Step 1: Affirmations

The first step in my three-step programme is to repeat a series of positive affirmations. When practiced consistently, affirmations can change the way you think about yourself and the world. You can repeat your affirmations regularly throughout the day and call on them in moments of vulnerability. When you are tempted to scour your oven for the third time in a month, or find yourself scrubbing away at a stain that nobody will notice, or when you feel an overwhelming desire to decant all your pantry items into artisanal glass jars, these affirmations will bring you back from the brink.

Please note that, for best results, these affirmations should be printed out individually in a bold but delicate font against an inspirational background – preferably a sunrise, the horizon, a calm ocean, or a baby guinea pig wearing a hat. (This last one isn't especially inspirational, but I promise you, if you google it, it's really, really cute.)

Affirmations to reprogramme the mess-challenged mind
1. Disarray is OK!
2. I don't need an aspirational pantry to be loved.
3. A clean pot never boils.
4. Near enough is good enough, but not even close is better.

5. There's no point vacuuming over spilt milk.
6. I clean to live; I don't live to clean.
7. Mess is the spice of life!
8. A woman's work is never done, so why try?
9. Better cluttered than sorry.
10. I don't sweat the small stuff. Or clean it.
11. Every dust cloud has a silver lining.
12. A journey of a thousand miles starts with a nice cup of tea and a lie down.
13. I choose mess!

Step 2: Exposure therapy

The second step in my three-step programme is exposure therapy.

For many people living with neatness, mess is not just an aversion, it is an outright phobia. When confronted with mess, they experience the emotional and physical responses associated with fear: racing heart, sweaty palms and a frantic desire to get rid of the source of the terror.

Now, I suffer from a phobia myself, so I feel tremendous empathy for their suffering. I am pathologically afraid of mice, and can barely even type those four letters without a serious elevation of blood pressure.

The difference, of course, is that mess cannot hurt you, whereas mice pose a very real threat to my life. A mouse could scuttle over my shoe, in which case I'd have to hack off my foot, and I could easily bleed to death from the wound.

Still, the treatment for both phobias is the same, even though my fear is clearly more justified and reasonable. (I mean, a mouse could hide behind a curtain and jump out at me at night, and I could totally have a heart attack and die.) When a person fears a scary thing (like a mouse) or a not-at-all scary thing (like mess), they try to avoid it, which makes the fear and the stress reaction grow. This treatment is a gradual exposure to the thing so that it eventually loses its power, and the fear and need for avoidance diminish.

A plan for gradual exposure to mice is very complicated. You need to catch the mice, then train them to scurry into a room for just a moment and obediently scurry out immediately afterwards. But a plan for gradual exposure to mess is quite simple. Over a period of days and weeks, you insert small messes into your home, steadily increasing their size and intensity. You will need to leave these messes alone, sitting with your discomfort, no matter how desperately you wish to clean. By the end of your course of therapy, you will have increased your tolerance of imperfection, and banished your phobia of mess forever.

A graduated plan for exposure to mess

Step 1: Place a single blueberry in the middle of your living-room floor.

Step 2: Go to your colour-coded bookshelf and swap a red book with a blue book.

Step 3: Go for an entire week without making your bed. (Mum, please don't do this without checking with the cardiologist first.)

Step 4: Eat a taco on your couch without using a plate.

Step 5: Put a cat and a few balls of wool into a room and close the door.

Step 6: Open a new packet of flour and sneeze in its general direction.

Step 7: Do some finger painting with a toddler at your dining-room table.

Step 8: Give a child some glue, some borax and a few bottles of food colouring, and challenge them to make rainbow slime.

Step 9: Make schnitzels from scratch – with egg, flour and breadcrumbs – and fry them up in hot oil, without cleaning up as you go along.

Step 10: Put on fake tan in the middle of your lounge room.

Step 11: Borrow a small dog and take it to the park on a rainy day, then let it run around in your living room. If you can't find a small dog, an extremely large cat will do.

Step 12: Throw a house party for a bunch of teens, with pizza and plenty of beer.

Step 13: You are now cured (or medicated).

> **Postscript:** For the record, I did not do exposure therapy for my fear of mice. It is simply too risky. A mouse could run up my arm and crawl into my ear and burrow deep inside my brain, and that would kill me. Better I just avoid mice.

Step 3: Avert your eyes

The final step in my patented [definitely not patented –Ed] three-step programme is to learn to avert your eyes.

I learned the power of harnessing a blind eye when I moved into my current apartment. I have a north-facing apartment with glass sliding doors opening onto a balcony, and for a couple of hours in the morning I am literally blinking in the dazzling sunlight. The real estate agent raved about this sunlight. Apparently it is a rare and much sought-after commodity.

Well, I do not like this blazing sunlight. This sunlight does very bad things.

When the sun is flooding through the glass doors and into my living room, every smear, every smudge and every streak on the glass is highlighted in excruciating detail. To add insult to injury, the sun hits the parquet floors at an angle, accentuating each tiny speck of dust and every single footprint. My apartment looks perfectly satisfactory by late morning, but from sun-up to 8 am it is a horror story.

During my first few weeks in this apartment, I was appalled by the view in the mornings. I would go to sleep in an acceptably clean home and wake up to a building site. On several occasions I mopped the floors before breakfast, certain that home invaders had managed to coat the living room in dust while we were all fast asleep in our beds. Once or twice, I was so disgusted by my windows that I washed them before I'd had my coffee.

And let me tell you: I don't do *anything* before I've had my coffee.

It took several months of being confronted with the magnification of my mess to understand that it was a mere trick of the light, and that it would pass in a couple of hours. I learned to firmly avert my eyes from the whole smeary, dusty mess until the sun had settled into a more aesthetically kind position. By 9 or 10 am, the smears and dust were still there, but I couldn't see them as clearly. This worked perfectly well for me.

Once I learned to turn a blind eye, I practised this tactic for all aspects of household management. Turning a blind eye is simple, effective, portable and, best of all, perfectly free. The pantry is messy? Shut the pantry door and you won't notice! The bed isn't made? Leave the bedroom immediately! There is a pile of laundry on the floor in the hall? Avert your eyes from the hallway! Look out the window instead!

If used judiciously, the capacity to turn a blind eye will serve you as well in life as it does in your home. Turn your gaze away from anything that causes you needless pain, like Photoshopped beauty influencers, unsavoury politicians, TV shows that marry people at first sight, friends who brag about their perfect kids, pushy sales assistants, fad diets, mean people on the internet, and coriander.

There are so many things to look at in life, and so many positive things to consider. Avert your eyes and your thoughts from those things that don't serve you. Eventually, the light will move away from them, and everything will look better.

TWELVE

The glass is always cleaner on the other side: banishing judgement

When you feel judged

Most people do not care at all about the state of your home. However, most people does not equal all people, and occasionally you will sense judgement oozing from the pores of a visitor.

When this happens, first consider that you could be misinterpreting their signals. You might be sure that your guest is staring in horror at your pile of dirty laundry, when really they are thinking, *God, I need to pee so badly*, or *Damn, I forgot to call the dentist*, or *I'm starving, I hope she offers me some cake*.

Still, it is possible that your guest is hyper-critical, or what psychologists refer to as 'judgey-wudgey'. They may have very strong thoughts on how you should live your life and how you should run your home and your family.

Now, hyper-critical people will judge everyone for something; that's just how their brains are wired. If they're not judging you for your mess then they will judge you for your clothes, or for your weight, or for the colour of your hair. They will judge you for your politics, or for your décor, or for your taste in books, or for your shyness, or your raunchy humour, or your car. They will judge you for letting your kids eat biscuits before dinner, or for not letting your kids eat biscuits at all. They will judge you for working too hard, or for not working hard enough, or they will judge you for your choice of career. They will judge you for your relationship, or for not having a relationship, or for having no kids, or too many.

What sad little lives these poor people must have! Let me block them on social media right now.

There are many ways to deal with a hyper-critical person:

1. *Take their judgement as gospel and get upset.*

   I know plenty of people do this, but it gives Judgey McJudgeFace far more power than they deserve. I mean, who elected them boss of your world? Why does their opinion hold so much weight?

2. *Get angry and kick them out of your home.*
    I can see how this would be deeply satisfying, and you could then tick 'kick someone out of my house' off your bucket list. But anger is very tiring, and you're still giving the judgey person way too much power.

3. *Let the judgement slide over you like the Teflon you so rarely clean.*
    I like this one. After all, judgements are mere opinions, and opinions aren't objective facts. It matters not one iota what other people think about your life; it only matters what you think about yourself. If your messy house is upsetting you, then do something about it. If your messy house is upsetting your visitor, then that is their problem entirely.

4. *Turn on some music and perform an interpretive dance for your visitor, expressing your utter lack of regard for their judgement.*
    This is quite clearly the best possible option.

Of course, the worst judgements don't come from other people; they come from ourselves. If you have a tendency to judge yourself, it can help enormously to stop comparing yourself to others. After all, there will always be people greater and lesser – and cleaner and messier – than you.

There are people walking the Earth who can work full time, raise six or seven kids, stay fit and well groomed, and still keep a sparkling clean home. Just as some humans are freakishly attractive, others are freakishly competent.

But there are many more people just plodding along in a barely restrained thrum of chaos. There are plenty of people whose houses are constantly messy, whose bedsheets are always crumpled and whose clothes are rarely ironed. I know this to be true because I am one of those people. If you need to compare yourself to another person, compare yourself to me.

When you feel messy

Some days, you just wake up and feel messy.

Actually, scrap that. I shouldn't speak for you. You might be one of those people who is always in control, who always looks immaculate, and whose home is always perfect. If so, I am genuinely happy for you. Also? I will not be following you on Instagram.

I, on the other hand, frequently feel messy, and this rarely has anything to do with the state of my house. I can feel quite calm when my house is completely shambolic, and totally messed up when my house is relatively clean. Mess, my friends, is a state of mind.

If you're having a messy day, start by asking yourself what it is that you feel messy about. Is the mess really inside your home, or is the mess inside your head?

If the mess is inside your home, and it's a kind of mess that bothers you, try tidying up just a little. Embracing the life-changing magic of a little bit of mess doesn't mean living in filth; it means giving up perfectionism and aspirational pantries.

If the mess is inside your head, then your time might be better spent tidying up your thoughts. There are a few things you can do to help yourself feel less chaotic, and none of them involve picking up a turbo mop or bleach.

How to tidy up a messy mind

1. Sit down, grab a pen and a piece of paper, and write down a list of everything that's worrying you. Putting your worries down on paper helps to clear them out of your head.

2. Write a list of everything you need to do, but don't panic! You don't need to do everything on the list! Just the act of creating a to-do list will help you to feel immediately more in control.

3. Have a nice cup of tea to remind yourself
   that you are worthy of care and compassion.
   (Unless you don't like tea, in which case please
   don't, as it will have the opposite effect. Try
   coffee, or hot chocolate, or Coke Zero, or
   juice.)

4. Remind yourself that life is messy. Human beings
   are messy. Relationships are messy. Parenting is
   extremely messy! There is so much in life that we
   can't control. We all drive ourselves mad trying
   to impose order, to be perfect, to keep all the
   balls in the air, to get everything done. We need
   to give ourselves permission to be flawed. It is
   perfectly OK to make a mess.

5. Go onto your social-media accounts and
   unfollow everyone who makes you feel bad
   about your life. Unfollow the beauty influencers,
   and the fitness influencers, and the #homeinspo
   influencers, and the #blessed influencers, and
   the hot bikini influencers. Unfollow that actor
   who talks about manifesting her good fortune,
   the friend who brags about her three perfect
   children, and your cousin who leaves conspiracy
   theorist comments on your posts. Say goodbye
   to these people! Bid them adieu! Farewell!
   They will stop existing the moment you press

Unfollow, and your social-media feeds will feel so much more empowering.

6. Remind yourself that nobody is perfect. No one you have ever met has a perfect life. None of the influencers you follow is perfectly happy. Everyone has anxieties and insecurities and regrets and pain. Everyone has days when they feel like they're completely failing. Everyone has challenges and irritations in their relationships. There are people with beautiful homes who have terrible marriages. There are people with great careers who have serious problems with their kids. There are people with fame and money who are profoundly lonely. Absolutely everyone is messy in some fundamental way. Don't get down on yourself for not being perfect. You are one of a long, proud line of people with fantastically messy lives.

CONCLUSION

The five stages of mess

SOME PEOPLE ARE MESSY from the moment they are born (or from the moment they can fling their toy onto the floor instead of placing it neatly back on the shelf). These people are glorious, sentient hurricanes of chaos. They are the living embodiments of the joy of mess.

Few of us can boast such a proud record of being consistently, unwaveringly untidy. Most of you reading this book will have kept your homes neat for at least brief periods of time. Perhaps you moved into a new house and worked very hard to keep your home perfectly clean for the first few months. Perhaps you did a renovation and experienced the joys of freshly painted walls and a bright, shiny new kitchen. Or maybe you did a spring clean on your home a while back and it stayed immaculately tidy for days.

But then, a week, or a month, or even a year down the track, your pristine home went to hell. You woke up and realised there was caked-on grease in the oven, and mould in the shower, and a dent in the bedroom wall – and you thought, hang on, how did I get here?

Though you may not have been consciously aware of your journey, becoming messy is a spiritual process. In her ground-breaking work, *The Five Stages of Mess*, Monica Chandler-Ross identified five distinct stages of mess: Denial, Anger, Bargaining, Depression and Acceptance. To help you to understand your own sacred journey, I have reproduced these five stages for you below.

Editor's note: Our fact-checker cannot find any evidence of the work of Ms Chandler-Ross.

Stage 1: Denial

The first stage of mess begins when your house is still clean. You are absolutely committed to maintaining it that way, and you deny to yourself and to others that you are ever going to mess it up. 'This time I am going to keep it perfect!' you say, and you absolutely believe it. You rush to clean every finger mark on the wall. All the dishes are put away before they even touch the counter. The laundry is folded as soon as it comes off the line. The pantry is colour-coded. The polished floors gleam.

Stage Two: Anger

Cracks begin to appear in your domestic perfection, and it is *not* your fault, and it makes you cross. Your partner chips the paint as he's moving a chair away from the table, and for God's sake, could he be more careless and annoying? The kids keep leaving their crap on the kitchen table, and is it really so hard to put things away when you've finished with them? Oh, and the cat keeps scratching away at the furniture, and who decided to get a stupid cat anyway?

Stage Three: Bargaining

Right. You're going to get this house back in order. You draw up a schedule and delegate chores to all the members of your household. You spend half an hour choosing fonts, you colour-code the schedule, and then you print it out and post it resolutely on the fridge. You offer your kids rewards if they complete their tasks on time, and you inform your partner sternly that 'Things are going to change around here!'

Stage Four: Depression

Well, the kids couldn't care less about your schedule. They glance at it once, say, 'I'm not doing that for a measly five dollars!' and then never look at it again. Your partner desultorily wipes the shower screen once or twice, and then must be asked three times to use a coaster under his coffee mug. No one cares. No one helps you with the cleaning. It's all hopeless. What's the point? You give up.

Stage Five: Acceptance

Mess, shmess. What even is 'tidy' anyway? The toilet is presentable. You changed the bedsheets sometime last month. You have clean undies for tomorrow. The pantry doors are firmly closed. You make yourself a nice cup of tea and have a nap on the couch. You are relaxed. You are at peace. You have embraced the magic of mess.

This, my friends, is what I wish for you.

ACKNOWLEDGEMENTS

FIRST AND FOREMOST, THANK you to my publisher, Mary Rennie, for recognising me as the aspirational home influencer I am. Thanks to Andy Warren for the fabulous cover, and to Shannon Kelly and the rest of the team at HarperCollins for bringing this book to life. It's been a delight working with all of you.

Thank you to my agents, Pippa Masson and Caitlan Cooper-Trent from Curtis Brown, for all your guidance and care.

A huge thanks to Saachi Owen for the brilliant illustrations. I adore them.

And to my parents and kids, who supported me as I wrote this book during lockdown, I couldn't have made this mess without you.